(L)(B)

LITTLE, BROWN and COMPANY

NEW YORK BOSTON

SHARK

by IRA MARCKS

COLOR ASSISTANCE by EMILY ARGOFF

About This Book

This book was edited by Andrea Colvin and designed by Ching N. Chan. The production was supervised by Bernadette Flinn, and the production editor was Lindsay Walter-Greaney.
The text was set in Amity Island, and the display type is Amity Island.

This book is a work of fiction. Names, characters, places, and incidents are the product of the author's imagination or are used fictitiously. Any resemblance to actual events, locales, or persons, living or dead, is coincidental.

Copyright © 2021 by Ira Marcks
Coloring assistance by Emily Argoff. Interior lettered by Paul Banks.

Cover illustration copyright © 2021 by Ira Marcks. Cover design by Ira Marcks and Ching N. Chan.
Cover copyright © 2021 by Hachette Book Group, Inc.

Hachette Book Group supports the right to free expression and the value of copyright. The purpose of copyright is to encourage writers and artists to produce the creative works that enrich our culture.

The scanning, uploading, and distribution of this book without permission is a theft of the author's intellectual property.
If you would like permission to use material from the book (other than for review purposes), please contact permissions@hbgusa.com. Thank you for your support of the author's rights.

Little, Brown and Company
Hachette Book Group
1290 Avenue of the Americas, New York, NY 10104
Visit us at LBYR.com

First Edition: May 2021

Little, Brown and Company is a division of Hachette Book Group, Inc.
The Little, Brown name and logo are trademarks of Hachette Book Group, Inc.

The publisher is not responsible for websites (or their content) that are not owned by the publisher.

Image of Snoopy and Woodstock keychain on page 231 © 2021 Peanuts Worldwide LLC

Library of Congress Cataloging-in-Publication Data
Names: Marcks, Ira, author.
Title: Shark summer / Ira Marcks.
Description: First edition. | New York: Little, Brown and Company, 2021. | Summary: When a Hollywood director starts filming a blockbuster action film on the otherwise sleepy island of Martha's Vineyard, thirteen-year-old Gayle and her friends set out to make their own film and solve an island mystery.
Identifiers: LCCN 2020032650 | ISBN 9780316461382 (hardcover) | ISBN 9780759555754 (ebook) | ISBN 9780759555761 (ebook) | ISBN 9780759555785 (ebook other)
Subjects: LCSH: Graphic novels. | CYAC: Graphic novels. | Motion pictures—Fiction. | Martha's Vineyard (Mass.)—Fiction.
Classification: LCC PZ7.7.M3378 Sh 2021 | DDC 741.5/973—dc23
LC record available at https://lccn.loc.gov/2020032650

ISBNs: 978-0-316-46138-2 (hardcover), 978-0-316-46144-3 (pbk.), 978-0-316-46139-9 (ebook), 978-0-7595-5576-1 (ebook), 978-0-7595-5575-4 (ebook)

Printed in China.

1010
Hardcover: 10 9 8 7 6 5 4 3 2 1
Paperback: 10 9 8 7 6 5 4 3

To Marie

and our summers together.

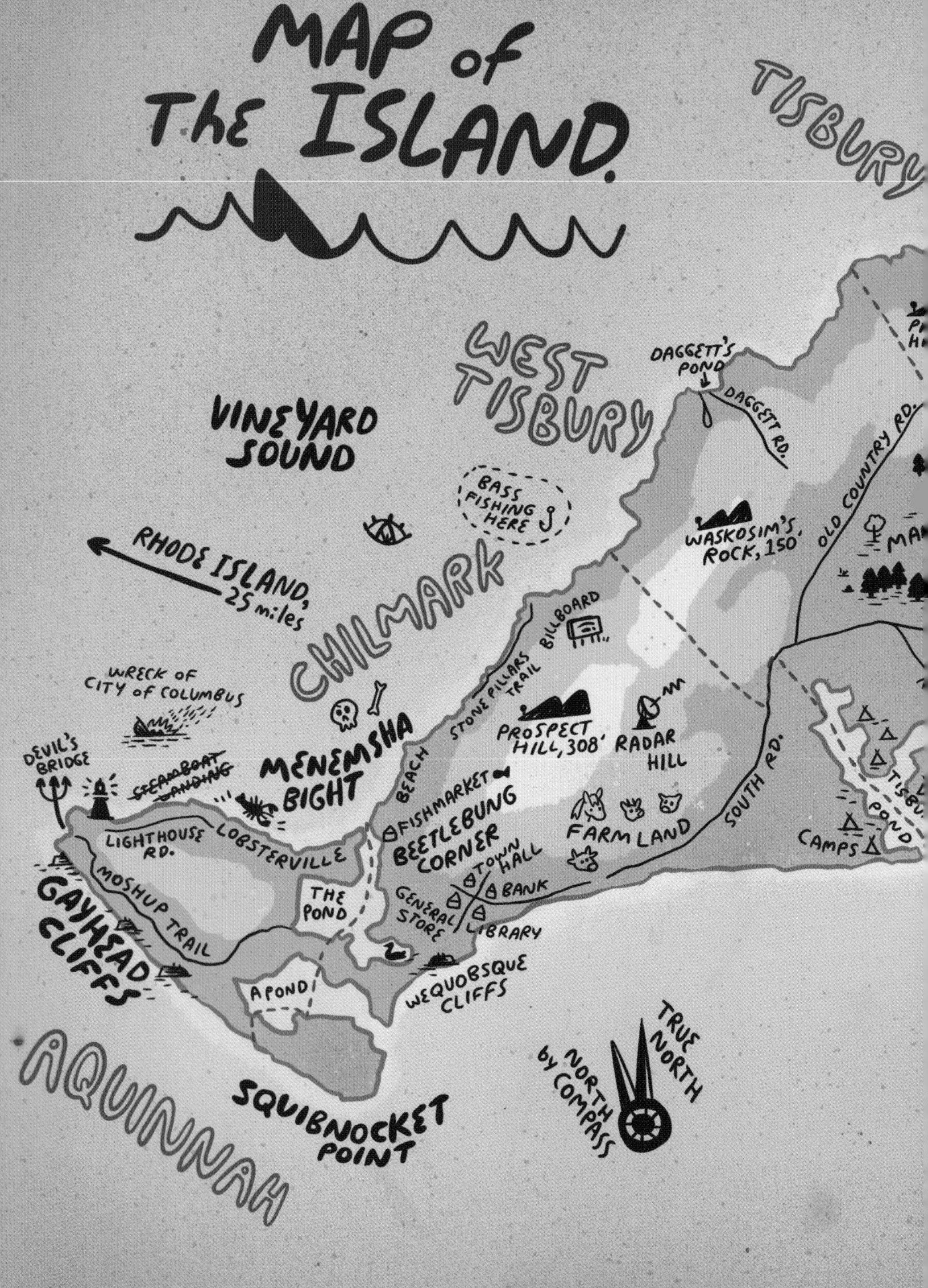

MAP of THE ISLAND

TISBURY

WEST TISBURY

VINEYARD SOUND

DAGGETT'S POND

DAGGETT RD.

BASS FISHING HERE

OLD COUNTRY RD.

WASKOSIM'S ROCK, 150'

RHODE ISLAND, 25 miles

CHILMARK

BILLBOARD

STONE PILLARS TRAIL

WRECK OF CITY of COLUMBUS

PROSPECT HILL, 308'

RADAR HILL

MENEMSHA BIGHT

DEVIL'S BRIDGE

~~STEAMBOAT LANDING~~

BEACH

FISHMARKET

BEETLEBUNG CORNER

FARM LAND

SOUTH RD.

TISBURY POND

CAMPS

LIGHTHOUSE RD.

LOBSTERVILLE

TOWN HALL

BANK

GENERAL STORE

LIBRARY

THE POND

MOSHUP TRAIL

GAYHEAD CLIFFS

A POND

WEQUOBSQUE CLIFFS

TRUE NORTH

NORTH by COMPASS

AQUINNAH

SQUIBNOCKET POINT

OAK BLUFFS
MASSACHUSETTS, 18 miles
MADDIE'S LIGHTHOUSE
EAST CHOP LIGHTHOUSE
VINEYARD HAVEN
SHARK CITY
HAVEN HARBOR
DAGGETT AVE.
NEW YORK AVE.
OAK BLUFFS HARBOR
GOLF COURSE
LAGOON POND
HARTHHAVEN PIER
(GRAND) ATLANTIC OCEAN
CAPE POGE LIGHTHOUSE
??
GOLF COURSE
LAGOON HEIGHTS??
VINEYARD HAVEN RD.
SENGEKONTACKET POND
COVE
MEMORIAL BRIDGE
CORRELLUS STATE FOREST
OCEAN HEIGHTS
EEL POND
LITTLE BEACH
CAPE POGE POND
VINEYARD AIRPORT
YET ANOTHER GOLF COURSE
LEX'S PLACE!
DUKE'S
LIGHTHOUSE BEACH
VINEYARD PREP
WATER ST.
BLACK CAT!
BEACH CLUB
OWN - WEST TISBURY RD.
MORNING GLORY FARM
MYTOI WALKING PATH
BLUEGILLS STADIUM
SPRINGS
SAMPSON HILL, 90'
TURKEY LAND
KATAMA RD.
CHAPPAQUIDDICK ISLAND
CAMPS
COVE
SWIMMING PLACE
GREAT POND
OLD TOWN PLAINS *
THE BAY
POND
BLUFF!
LAND BANK BEACH
*1801
SOUTH BEACH
OYSTER POND
NANTUCKET, 19 miles
EDGARTOWN (AMITY)
IF FOUND PLEASE RETURN TO ELIJAH JONES at the GRAND ATLANTIC HOTEL!

YOUTH FASTPITCH CHAMPIONSHIP
GIVE 'EM THE BLUES
BLUE STREAK
GO GILLS
BLUEGILLS

WOOSH
YER OUT!

SHE'S UNSTOPPABLE!
WHAT AN ARM!
THAT'S MY GIRL!
BLUE!
STREAK!
BLUE!
STREAK!
BLUE!
STREAK!

TIME OUT!
BRIAR

GAYLE?
LEX?
WHAT ARE YOU DOING?

I HAD TO SEE WHAT IT LOOKED LIKE OUT HERE.
PRETTY AMAZING, RIGHT?

THE BLUEGILLS HAVE NEVER MADE IT TO A CHAMPIONSHIP.
NOT UNTIL YOU SHOWED UP.
WHAT ARE WE WAITING FOR?
LET'S MAKE HISTORY.

LET'S DO IT.
YOUR CAPTAIN NEEDS THREE STREAKERS RIGHT DOWN THE MIDDLE.
ONE!
TWO!
THREE!

AYE, AYE, CAPTAIN.

NO FREAKING WAY.

SOMEONE GET UNDER THAT BALL!

I GOT IT!

ACT 1

GAYLE!

TIME TO WAKE UP!

BOSTON ACADEMY

HEY, KIDDO! YOU ALIVE OR WHAT?
NOT SURE YET.

ARE YOU PUTTING ON MAKEUP?
I SURE AM!

BUT WE WERE SUPPOSED TO PAINT THE SHOP TODAY.
YOU'RE STILL PAINTING.

THEN WHAT ARE YOU DOING?
I GOT A CALLBACK FOR A PART IN THE MOVIE!
SMUDGE

IT'S A SMALL ROLE. BUT THIS MOVIE STUDIO PAYS BIG MONEY, KIDDO. WE CAN'T PASS IT UP.

BUT I CAN'T PAINT ALONE! LOOK AT ME— I'M USELESS!

YOU'RE NOT USELESS. YOU'RE SCARED YOU MIGHT SEE LEX OUT THERE.

YOU CAN'T HIDE IN THE ATTIC ALL SUMMER, KIDDO. THE REAL WORLD IS CALLING YOU.

WHAT REAL WORLD?!
THERE'S A MOVIE SET OUTSIDE OUR WINDOW!

BESIDES, LEX IS AVOIDING ME, TOO.
YOU'RE BOTH BEING ABSURD.

MOM . . .
IS IT MY FAULT WE LOST THE GAME?

WHAT HAVE I BEEN SAYING SINCE THE DAY WE MOVED TO THE ISLAND?

"IF IT'S WORTH DOING, IT'S WORTH THE RISK."

YOU TOOK A RISK WITH THAT POP FLY. WAS IT WORTH IT?
YEAH.

THAT'S ALL THAT MATTERS.

OH GEESH, I GOTTA GO. THEY WANT ME THERE BY SEVEN FOR COSTUMING.
HEY, WAIT!
WHAT AM I SUPPOSED TO DO?

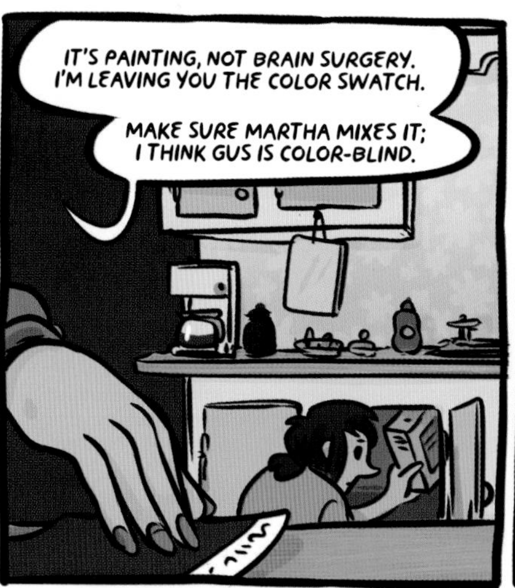

IT'S PAINTING, NOT BRAIN SURGERY. I'M LEAVING YOU THE COLOR SWATCH.
MAKE SURE MARTHA MIXES IT; I THINK GUS IS COLOR-BLIND.

HMM . . .
TELL THE DUKES I'LL SETTLE UP LATER.

SO, WHAT'S THE PART THEY WANT YOU FOR?

I'M PLAYING A MOM WHOSE KID GETS EATEN BY A SHARK.
WISH ME LUCK!

WHAT THE HECK IS THIS MOVIE?

HARDWARE
HI, MRS. DUKE! CAN I ORDER TWO CANS OF THIS COLOR, PLEASE?
DUKE'S HARDWARE
COMING RIGHT UP!

PAINTBRUSH, CHECK.

LUNCH, CHECK.
COSMIC BAR
CHOMP!
CHOMP! ..CHOCOLATE BAR...

GOOD MORNING, MR. DUKE! MOM SAID SHE'LL SETTLE UP LATER, OK?
THAT'S FINE. PAINTING THE CREAMERY TODAY, I SEE.
KEYS

SURE AM. JUST A FEW FINISHING TOUCHES BEFORE THE GRAND OPENING! YOU'LL BE THERE, RIGHT?
OF COURSE! I'M ALWAYS THERE FOR BIG ISLAND NEWS. WHEN'S THE BIG DAY?

NOT SURE EXACTLY...
HEY, WHAT HAPPENED TO MY PICTURE?
OH, WELL...
THOSE MOVIE FOLKS FILMED A SCENE IN HERE YESTERDAY.

AND THEY TOLD YOU TO TAKE DOWN MY PICTURE?
EVERY STREAK COMES TO AN END, GAYLE. AND AFTER WHAT HAPPENED AT THE CHAMPIONSHIP...
BLUE GILLS BLUE STREAK!

DIDN'T THINK WE'D WANT IT CAUGHT FOREVER ON FILM.
ZODAK
DUKE'S HARDWARE
OH, RIGHT. I GET IT.

DIDN'T REALIZE I MARRIED THE ISLAND HISTORIAN.
EH.

DUKE'S HARDWARE
OPEN

HEY, KID!
HUH?

WATCH WHERE YOU'RE GOING.

SORRY!

WATCH THE CURB, NUMBSKULLS!
THOSE LIGHTING FIXTURES ARE WORTH MORE THAN THE TWO OF YOU COMBINED!
HEY, CARL. HOW ABOUT LENDING A HAND, HUH?
NO CAN DO. UNION RULES.
GOOD TO KNOW WHERE WE STAND, EDDY.
HARDWARE
#1
BANAVISION
B-35

THE BEACH IS CLOSED? WHAT THE HECK HAPPENED?
IT'S A PROP, KID. IT AIN'T REAL.
NO SWIMMING
HAZARDOUS AREA
BEACH CLOSED
By order Amity P.D.

IT SURE LOOKS REAL.
YEAH, THAT'S KINDA THE POINT.

HOW LONG DOES IT TAKE TO MAKE A MOVIE?
HEH, THERE'S NO EASY ANSWER TO THAT QUESTION.
THE STUDIO WANTS US TO WRAP UP PRODUCTION BY THE END OF SUMMER. BUT IT'S NOT UP TO US. NOT REALLY.

IT'S UP TO BRUCE THE SHARK.

WHOA! YOU HAVE A REAL SHARK?
YEAH, HE'S A REAL PAIN IN THE—
YOUR BREAK IS OVER, CARL! GET BACK TO WORK!

DOCK ST.
COFFEE SHOP
OPEN

KELSEY'S
BICYCLE
RENTAL

GALLERY
ALL RATES DOUBLE
7:30 TO MIDNITE

LOBSTER
NO
ALL
MEAT
ROLL

WAMPUM
JEWELRY
LOCAL ART

PSYCHIC
PALM
TAROT

SEAGLASS
SUMMER SALE
SIGH.
BLACK CAT CREAMERY
ISLA GALL
SUPPORT VINEYARD ARTISTS
GALLERY

BLACK CAT CREAMERY

WHAT A STRIKING COLOR!

HEY, THANKS!
MOM CALLS IT HER GOOD-LUCK COLOR.

A FAMILY BUSINESS VENTURE! HOW EXCITING! ARE YOU NEW TO THE VINEYARD, THEN?

YEAH, WE MOVED FROM BOSTON IN DECEMBER.
ISN'T THAT DELIGHTFUL?!

YOU DRESS REALLY NICE! ARE YOU AN ACTOR IN THE MOVIE?
YOU FLATTER ME! NO, I'M BUT A HUMBLE JOURNALIST.

THE NAME IS TERRY JONES. I REPORT ON CULTURE FOR HAPPENINGS MAGAZINE.
THE NAME IS GAYLE BRIAR. I'M THE PITCHER FOR THE VINEYARD BLUEGILLS.

NOT TO BE RUDE, BUT WHAT ARE YOU DOING HERE? MARTHA'S VINEYARD ISN'T WHAT I'D CALL "HAPPENING."
YOU MUST SEE IT AS I SEE IT, MS. BRIAR.

NOW,
PICTURE THIS—

EACH JULY, PEOPLE FLOCK HERE FROM THE MAINLAND.

THEY WALK THE BRICK-LINED STREETS.

THEY EAT A LOBSTER ROLL . . .

DO SOME SHOPPING . . .

EXPLORE LOCAL CULTURE . . .

AND WATCH THE SUNSET WITH A GLASS OF WINE.

HOW 'BOUT AN ICE-CREAM CONE?
EVEN BETTER.

NEXT YEAR, THEY RETURN TO THE ISLAND EXPECTING IT ALL TO BE THE SAME.

A SUMMER THAT NEVER CHANGES.
PRECISELY.

SOUNDS KINDA BORING, HONESTLY.
AH!
BUT THIS SUMMER IS DIFFERENT!

SURELY YOU MUST KNOW ABOUT THE SHARK MOVIE.
KINDA.

I'M HERE TO TELL THE STORY OF A TIMELESS ISLAND OFF THE COAST OF MASSACHUSETTS THAT WAS FOREVER CHANGED BY HOLLYWOOD.

REALLY?
I MEAN, IT'S JUST A MOVIE.

THAT'S WHERE YOU ARE WRONG, MS. BRIAR. IT IS NOT "JUST A MOVIE."

THIS IS A . . .
MAJOR MOTION PICTURE.

MY SOURCES TELL ME . . .
GLOBAL STUDIOS IS INVESTING SEVEN MILLION DOLLARS IN THIS MOVIE.

WHOA, THAT'S A LOT!
IT IS MORE THAN A LOT.

SEVEN MILLION DOLLARS IS THE KIND OF MONEY THAT CAN CHANGE A PLACE.
BECAUSE IT'S THE KIND OF MONEY THAT CHANGES THE PEOPLE.

MARK MY WORDS—
THIS WILL BE A SUMMER TO REMEMBER!

BUT, LIKE, IN A GOOD WAY, RIGHT?

MR. JONES?

SORRY ABOUT MY DAD.
HE CAN GET OVERLY DRAMATIC.
THAT'S WHY HE'S A GREAT WRITER, I GUESS.

YEAH . . . HE KINDA FREAKED ME OUT.

HEY!
I KNOW YOU!
KNOW ME?

YOU'RE GAYLE BRIAR!

YOU HAVE A 24-1 RECORD; EIGHT NO-HITTERS AND TWO PERFECT GAMES.

YOU'RE A TWICE-RANKED DIVISION ONE CHAMPION PITCHER AND YOU'RE ONLY 13.

UH . . .
NOW YOU'RE STARTING TO FREAK ME OUT, TOO.

RIGHT, RIGHT!
SORRY, SORRY!

I'M ELIJAH JONES. WE GO TO BOSTON ACADEMY TOGETHER.

STRIKE THAT— USED TO GO TO BOSTON ACADEMY TOGETHER.
OK.
BUT WHY DO YOU KNOW MY STATS?

I FILM THE SPORTS EVENTS FOR THE ACADEMY, SO I WAS AT ALL OF YOUR GAMES.

YOUR FASTBALL IS AWESOME.

WAS AWESOME.

OUCH. WHAT HAPPENED?
LONG STORY.

IS IT A FRACTURE OR A SPRAIN? OR IT COULD BE BOTH. IS IT BOTH?
UM.

I GOTTA GET BACK TO WORK.

UGH!
SORRY AGAIN; I'M BEING NOSY, AREN'T I?

IT'S FINE, ELIJAH. I'VE JUST GOT A LOT OF WORK TO DO.

I WAS JUST SURPRISED TO SEE YOU LIVING ON MARTHA'S VINEYARD.
I'M STILL GETTING USED TO IT.

BUT MY MOM WANTED TO START HER OWN BUSINESS.
SO HERE WE ARE.

WHY HERE?
SHE'S ALWAYS WANTED TO LIVE ON THE ISLAND.

SHE'S COME HERE EVERY SUMMER SINCE SHE WAS A KID.

SHE ALWAYS TELLS ME HOW SHE'D GET UP AT DAWN TO COME DOWN AND WATCH THE FISHING BOATS LEAVING THE WHARF.

THE WHARF MUST HAVE LOOKED WAY DIFFERENT BACK THEN, HUH?
LESS PURPLE ICE-CREAM SHOPS, I BET.
THE WHARF
SHOPS · FOOD · ART

YOUR DAD SAID THIS MOVIE IS GONNA CHANGE THINGS EVEN MORE. THINK HE'S RIGHT?

I KNOW HE'S RIGHT. THAT'S WHY I'M MAKING . . .

A DOCUMENTARY!
YIKES.
SOUNDS LIKE HOMEWORK.

NO WAY —IT'S FUN!
I'M FOLLOWING MY DAD'S STORY; FILMING EVERY PLACE HE GOES AND THE PEOPLE HE TALKS TO.

AT THE END OF THE SUMMER WE'LL ENTER OUR FILM IN THE FILM FESTIVAL.

THE DIRECTOR OF SHARK! IS JUDGING THE COMPETITION, SO IT'S A GREAT NETWORKING OPPORTUNITY FOR AN ASPIRING CINEMATOGRAPHER.

THE BIG-DEAL HOLLYWOOD MOVIE; IT'S ACTUALLY CALLED SHARK?
NO, IT'S CALLED SHARK! WITH AN EXCLAMATION POINT.

SHARK!?
SHARK!

GOTCHA.
WELL, GOOD LUCK ON YOUR DOCUMENTARY, ELIJAH JONES.
THANK YOU.

UM, OK, SO I REALLY DO HAVE A LOT OF WORK TO DO.
HM.

I WAS THINKING YOU COULD SHOW ME AND MY DAD AROUND THE ISLAND TOMORROW.

WE NEED TO SHOOT SOME B-ROLL FOOTAGE; GATHER SHOTS OF ALL THE LOCAL LANDMARKS.

I ONLY MOVED HERE IN DECEMBER. I DON'T REALLY KNOW ANY ISLAND HISTORY.

NOT HISTORY. I JUST NEED SHOTS OF THE LIGHTHOUSES, BEACHES, FERRIES. YOU KNOW, TYPICAL ISLAND STUFF!

YOU CAN'T TAKE A HINT, CAN YOU?
I GET IT. YOU'RE A BUSINESS OWNER!
HERE'S MY PROPOSITION—

IF YOU SHOW US AROUND THE ISLAND, WE'LL FEATURE THE BLACK CAT CREAMERY IN THE DOCUMENTARY.
IT'LL BE GREAT EXPOSURE FOR YOU!

REALLY? YOU'D DO THAT?

IT'S A FAIR DEAL. WE BOTH WIN.

SHAKE ON IT?

WOW, OK. SO IT'S A DEAL.

TOWN HALL, TOMORROW 9 AM. BRING BIKES.
WE'LL BE THERE.

"UNTITLED ISLAND DOCUMENTARY"
★PRODUCTION SCHEDULE★
WEEK ONE
→DAY ONE←
9AM: TOWN HALL
ISLAND TOUR
W/ GAYLE BRIAR (BRING BIKES)

I'LL SEE YOU THEN!

GAYLE BRIAR.
DIVISION ONE CHAMPION PITCHER.

AND SMALL-BUSINESS OWNER.

IMPRESSIVE.

CREAMERY
COMING SOON!

LOBSTER
NO FILLER
ALL
MEAT
ROLL
GONE FISHIN'

WAMPUM
JEWELRY
LOCAL ART
CLOSED

PSYCHIC
PALM TAROT CRYSTAL

WORKING OVERTIME, I SEE.
MOM!

IT'S BEEN A CRAZY DAY!

YEAH? TELL ME.
OK, FIRST:
I MET THIS JOURNALIST NAMED TERRY JONES FROM HAPPENINGS MAGAZINE.

HE'S GOING TO TELL THE STORY OF A QUIET LITTLE ISLAND THAT WAS CHANGED BY HOLLYWOOD FOREVER.
WE'RE THE ISLAND, HE SAYS.

HE SAID, "MONEY CHANGES PEOPLE." NOT SURE WHAT THAT MEANS.
SOUNDS LIKE AN INTERESTING FELLOW.

THEN I MET HIS SON, ELIJAH, WHO GOES TO BOSTON ACADEMY. HE KNEW ALL MY PITCHING STATS, WHICH WAS WEIRD BUT KINDA FLATTERING.
ANYWAYS . . .

ELIJAH IS MAKING A MOVIE, I MEAN DOCUMENTARY, AND HE'S GOING TO PUT THE BLACK CAT CREAMERY IN IT! IT'LL BE GREAT EXPOSURE FOR US! SO COOL, RIGHT?
GREAT, KIDDO.

AND LAST BUT NOT LEAST!

IT'S LOOKING BEAUTIFUL, KIDDO.

MOM?
WHAT'S WRONG?

I DIDN'T GET THE PART.

BUT THEY WERE FITTING YOU FOR A COSTUME.
I KNOW.

THEY SAID I DIDN'T LOOK LIKE AN "AUTHENTIC ISLANDER."

WHAT'S THAT SUPPOSED TO MEAN?

DID THEY EXPECT ME TO SHOW UP WITH A LOBSTER TRAP AND WADERS?!

HEY, LOOK ON THE BRIGHT SIDE—NOW WE CAN FOCUS ON OUR GRAND OPENING!

I WAS THINKING— THE FIRST DAY OF SUMMER IS A WEEK AWAY. IT'S PERFECT TIMING.

OOH! WE CAN PRINT FLYERS ON PURPLE PAPER!

WHAT IF WE DID FREE KIDS' CONES ON THE FIRST DAY? IT'LL GET EVERYONE TALKING AND THEN—
WHOA, KIDDO! SLOW DOWN A SECOND.

SLOW DOWN?
IT'S ALMOST SUMMER!
I KNOW.

WE OWN AN ICE-CREAM SHOP.
I KNOW.
JUST LISTEN—

CHARLOTTE DAGGETT OFFERED ME A HOUSEKEEPING JOB AT HER HOTEL.

WHY IS LEX'S MOM OFFERING YOU A JOB?
WE JUST GOT TO TALKING . . .

YOU'RE NOT GOING TO TAKE IT, ARE YOU?

CHAR SAYS THE MOVIE STUDIO BOOKED A WHOLE WING OF THE HOTEL FOR THE NEXT THREE MONTHS. SHE SAYS THEY'RE BIG SPENDERS.

I'LL MAKE A KILLING IN TIPS!
I CAN'T BELIEVE THIS.

YOU MADE ME MOVE AWAY FROM MY CITY, AWAY FROM MY TEAM, AWAY FROM MY FRIENDS, TO OPEN AN ICE-CREAM SHOP ON AN ISLAND.

NOW YOU WANT TO BE A HOUSEKEEPER.

TRUST ME THE HOTEL GIG IS THE BEST CHOICE FOR US RIGHT NOW.

YOU'RE ALWAYS TALKING ABOUT TAKING RISKS.
I THOUGHT OPENING A CREAMERY WAS YOURS.

THAT WAS THE PLAN. AT THE TIME. BUT SOMETIMES, PLANS CHANGE.

NOTHING'S CHANGED!

EXCEPT . . .

EXCEPT ME.

MOM, THE EMERGENCY ROOM AFTER THE GAME. . .

WHAT DID IT COST TO FIX ME?
IT DOESN'T MATTER WHAT IT COST.

YOU'RE LYING! MONEY MATTERS!
NOW, DON'T GET UPSET.

OF COURSE I'M UPSET!
IT'S MY FAULT MY MOM IS GIVING UP HER DREAM!

FIRST MY ARM GOT SCREWED UP!

THEN YOUR DREAM GOT SCREWED UP!

ENOUGH, GAYLE.
NOTHING'S SCREWED UP.

THIS MORNING I ASKED YOU IF CHASING THAT POP FLY WAS WORTH THE RISK AND YOU TOLD ME:
YES.

I KNOW WHAT I SAID, BUT—

LISTEN TO ME.

I DON'T WANT YOU TO EVER APOLOGIZE FOR BELIEVING IN YOURSELF.

BUT—

NO BUTS! YOU GET ME?
YEAH.

I LOVE YOU, KIDDO.
LOVE YOU, TOO.

IT'S GOING TO WORK OUT AND THAT'S ALL THERE IS TO IT.

COME ON, I'LL HELP YOU CLEAN UP.
OK.

YOU KNOW, WHEN I WAS YOUR AGE, I'D SIT RIGHT HERE AND WATCH THE FISHING BOATS GO OUT.
I KNOW, MOM.

I'D STARE UNTIL THEY DISAPPEARED OVER THE HORIZON.

I WOULD GET THIS THRILL, YOU KNOW?

YEAH...

"LIKE YOU WERE STARING AT THE EDGE OF THE WORLD."

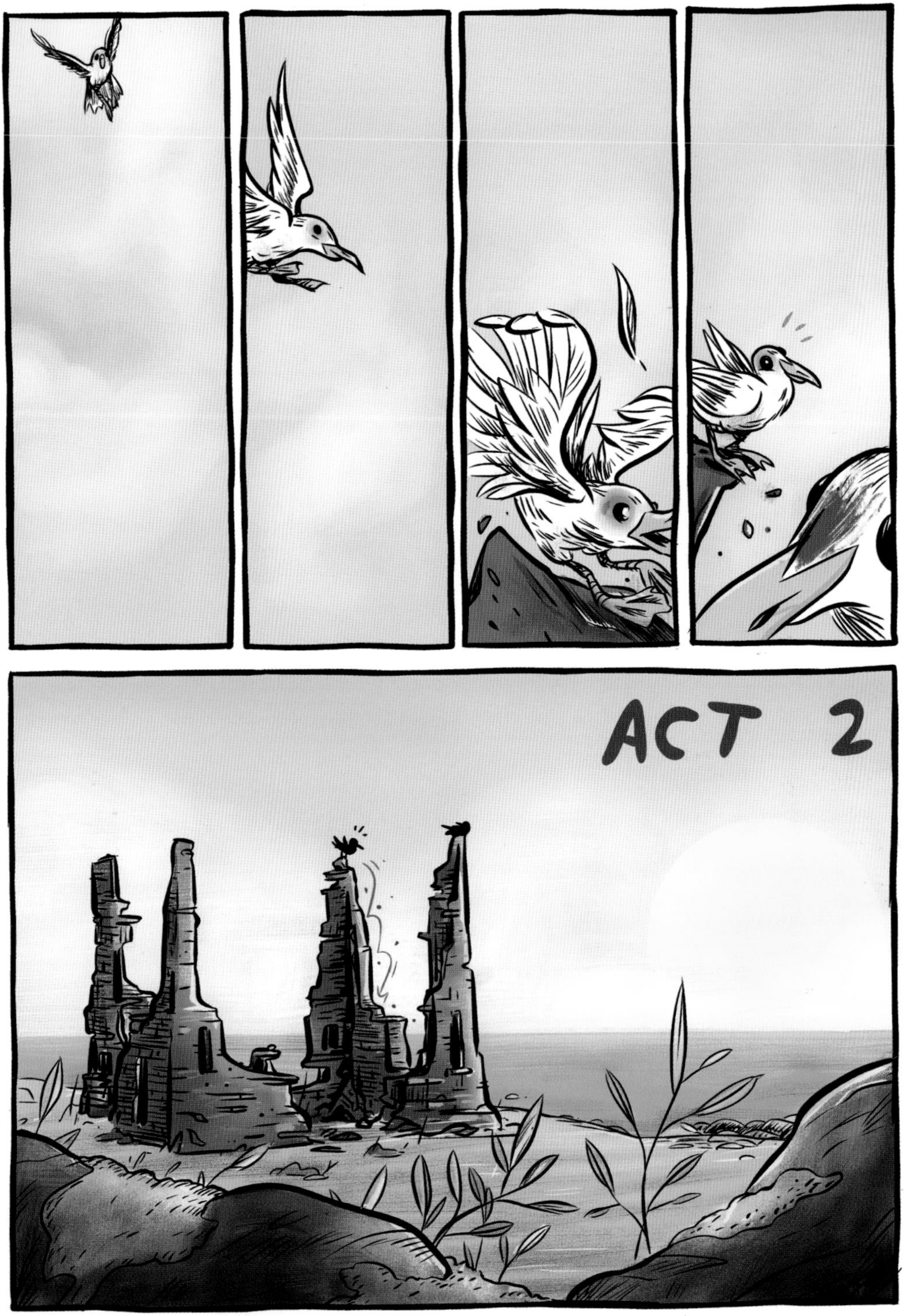

ACT 2

ELIJAH?!
EDGARTOWN TOWN HALL
SCREEE

9 AM.
RIGHT ON TIME.

GOOD MORNING!
THAT WAS QUITE AN ENTRANCE!

YEAH . . .
THE THROTTLE IS A LITTLE TOUCHY.

WHERE DID YOU GET THIS THING?
MY DAD BOUGHT IT FOR ME. SAID I NEEDED A WAY TO GET AROUND ON MY OWN.

I THOUGHT HE WAS COMING WITH US?
UM, HE'S NOT FEELING WELL.

AND OF COURSE YOU BROUGHT A MAP.
LET'S GET TO IT.
MARTHA'S VINEYARD IS 25 MILES FROM ITS LONGEST POINT EAST TO WEST AND 9 MILES NORTH TO SOUTH.

THIS ISLAND HAS APPROXIMATELY 96 SQUARE MILES TO EXPLORE.

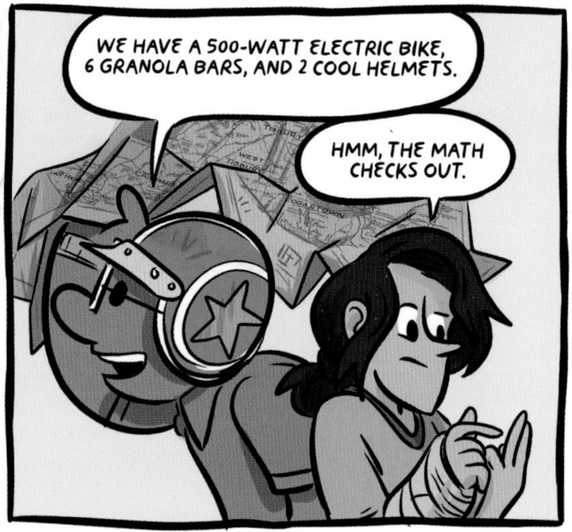
WE HAVE A 500-WATT ELECTRIC BIKE, 6 GRANOLA BARS, AND 2 COOL HELMETS.
HMM, THE MATH CHECKS OUT.

SORRY, OL' BLUE. YOU'LL HAVE TO WAIT BEHIND.

NOW, LISTEN, ELIJAH . . .
I JUST GOT OUT OF THE EMERGENCY ROOM. I DON'T WANT TO GO BACK.
NOTED.

EDGARTOWN TOWN HALL

WE'LL START AT THE WEST CHOP LIGHTHOUSE.
AH!
PERFECT.

GREAT MORNING LIGHT.
WHAT A SHOT!
16 · 8 · 4 · 1.9

HEY, CAN I TRY?
SURE...

THIS IS A ZODAK PRO-MATIC CAMERA.
IS IT NOW?

IT'S WATERPROOF, SHOOTS ON ZODACHROME COLOR FILM, HAS A MANUAL IRIS, AND I PUT A 5X ZOOM LENS FOR TODAY'S EXPEDITION.
VERY COOL.

AND VERY EXPENSIVE.
I'M BEING CAREFUL!

YOU SAID THIS THING'S GOT A ZOOM?

YES! IT'S CALLED THE DAS ZOOM-OBJEKTIV. IT'S A LIMITED EDITION FROM GERMANY!
OH MY GOSH, IT'S HER. I CAN'T BELIEVE IT!

WHO?
GHASTLY MADDIE. SHE LIVES IN THE OLD LIGHTHOUSE. LOOK! LOOK!

WHAT DO YOU THINK SHE'S DOING UP THERE?
IT LOOKS LIKE SHE'S READING A BOOK, GAYLE.

PROBABLY A SPELL BOOK. THE KIDS AT SCHOOL SAY SHE'S A VAMPIRE AND THE SUN BURNS HER SKIN AND SHE WANDERS AROUND GRAVEYARDS AT MIDNIGHT AND STUFF.

BUT MOST OF THE TIME HER PARENTS KEEP HER LOCKED IN THE TOWER LIKE SOME KINDA EVIL RAPUNZEL.

HEY, COME ON! MY CAMERA'S NOT FOR SPYING ON PEOPLE!

YOU SAID YOU WANTED TO SEE THE ISLAND LANDMARKS. GHASTLY MADDIE IS PRETTY MUCH THE BEST ONE.

NOW YOU'RE WEIRDING ME OUT!
FINE, LET'S MOVE ON.

HOW ABOUT WE GO INLAND?
TAKE A LEFT ON WEST TISBURY.

WHAT'S THAT AWFUL SMELL?
FARMLAND.
YOU GET USED TO IT.

HERE COMES A VERY IMPORTANT LOCAL LANDMARK!

BABY GOATS!
NOW THIS IS MORE LIKE IT!

I WANT MORE NATURE FOOTAGE. LET'S GET OFF THE MAIN ROAD.
THE MOSHUP TRAIL. IT'LL TAKE US THROUGH THE MARSHLANDS TO THE WEST COAST.

TRAIL

JUST A BIT CREEPY.

YOU WANT A VIEW? AQUINNAH CLIFFS, DEAD AHEAD!

WOW, THIS VAN CAME ALL THE WAY FROM . . . ONTARIO?

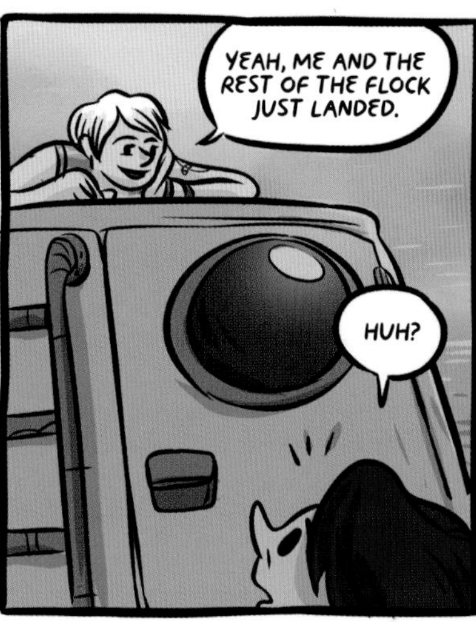
YEAH, ME AND THE REST OF THE FLOCK JUST LANDED.
HUH?

IT'S A CANADIAN GOOSE JOKE.
NAME'S ZHENELLE.
GAYLE.
ELIJAH.

WE WEREN'T TRYING TO SNOOP OR ANYTHING.
NO PROBLEM. WANNA GET A BETTER VIEW?

IT'S COOL. I DON'T BITE.

NICE VIEW, EH?

DO YOU HAVE NICE VIEWS WHERE YOU'RE FROM?
NOT LIKE THIS. I'M A MANITOBAN.

MAN-IT-OBAN.
IS THAT FROM *STAR TREK?*

YOU DON'T KNOW MUCH ABOUT CANADA, DO YOU?

I'M FROM WINNIPEG, MANITOBA— THE DEAD CENTER OF NORTH AMERICA. THE OCEAN IS 3,000 KILOMETERS IN EVERY DIRECTION.

ONE DAY, I JUST GOT SICK OF BEING LANDLOCKED.

SO I BOUGHT THIS OLD VAN AND JUST STARTED DRIVING TOWARDS THE EASTERN COASTLINE. WHEN I FINALLY HIT THE EDGE OF MASSACHUSETTS, I THOUGHT, WHY NOT HOP A FERRY TO MARTHA'S VINEYARD?

I KEPT GOING UNTIL I RAN OUT OF ROAD AND ENDED UP RIGHT HERE, JUST AS THE SUN WAS STARTING TO SET.

THAT SOUNDS PICTURE-PERFECT.

THAT WASN'T THE BEST PART. IT WAS AFTER, WHEN THE SKY STARTED TO DARKEN.

I REALIZED IT WOULD BE A MOONLESS NIGHT. THE SKY, THE LAND . . .

IT ALL STARTED TO DISAPPEAR.

YOU KIDS HAVE A NICE CAMERA . . .

BUT SOME THINGS CAN'T BE CAUGHT ON FILM.

YOU THINK YOU GOT SOME GOOD B-ROLL?
FOR THE FIRST DAY?
WELL BEYOND MY EXPECTATIONS.

WE MAKE A GOOD TEAM, GAYLE BRIAR.
THANKS, ELIJAH.
I REALLY NEEDED A DAY LIKE THIS.

IT'S NOT OVER YET!
IT'S NOT?

WHAT ARE WE DOING HERE?

THIS IS WHERE I'M STAYING FOR THE SUMMER!

YOU'RE STAYING AT THE GRAND ATLANTIC HOTEL?

HAPPENINGS MAGAZINE ALWAYS BOOKS MY DAD IN THE BEST HOTELS. AND WHEN THEY FIND OUT WHO HE IS, WE GET THE ROYAL TREATMENT.

COME ON IN — MY DAD LETS ME ORDER ANYTHING I WANT FROM ROOM SERVICE — OOF!
I GOTTA GET HOME.

GEESH, GAYLE! IS THIS PLACE HAUNTED OR SOMETHING?
HA HA, GOOD ONE! OK, I CAN WALK FROM HERE.

AH!

WELL, LOOK WHO IT IS!

THE BLUEGILLS' VERY OWN STAR PITCHER.

HELLO, MY DEAR.
HI, MRS. DAGGETT.

IT'S BEEN TOO LONG.
YOU'RE TAKING CARE OF YOURSELF, YES?
UH, YEAH.

FALL TRAINING WILL BE HERE BEFORE WE KNOW IT.

ARE YOU GOING TO SAY HELLO, LEX?

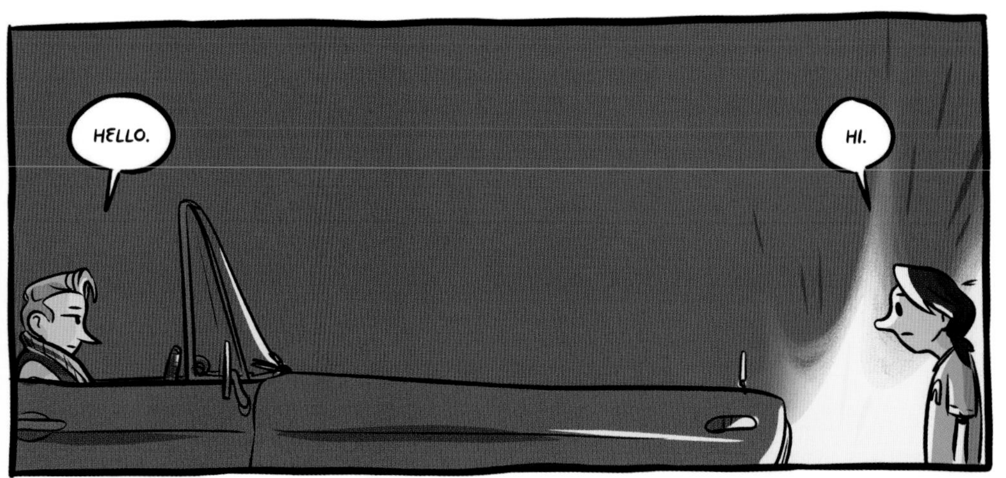
HELLO.
HI.

WELL, THIS IS COMPLETELY ABSURD.

I WILL NOT WATCH TWO BLUEGILLS STARE DAGGERS AT EACH OTHER. YOU'RE TEAMMATES, FOR GOODNESS' SAKE. ACT LIKE IT.

YOU'RE RIGHT, MOM.

YOU OK?
I'M OK.

THEN EVERYTHING'S ALL OK. I'LL SEE YOU AT PRACTICE.
TEAMMATE.

LEX, WHY DON'T YOU INVITE MS. BRIAR AND MR. JONES TO DINNER? I CAN RESERVE YOU A TABLE IN THE DINING ROOM.

I'M NOT ASKING, ALEXANDRIA!
MOM.

I'D LIKE IT IF YOU TWO WOULD JOIN ME FOR DINNER.
WE'RE IN! RIGHT, GAYLE?
UH,
ALL RIGHT.

HOW ARE YOU AND YOUR FATHER SETTLING IN? I TRUST THE ROOM IS TO YOUR LIKING?

IT'S AWESOME. THE BEDS ARE SO HUGE!
HUGE, INDEED! DID YOU KNOW THE GRAND ATLANTIC WAS ONE OF OUR COUNTRY'S FIRST LUXURY HOTELS?

IT WAS BUILT BY MY GREAT-GRANDMOTHER ALEXANDRIA DAGGETT. WE WORK HARD TO KEEP UP HER REPUTATION, DON'T WE, LEX?
WE SURE DO, MOM.

"There is no sight like that of the Grand Atlantic."

OH MY GOSH, THAT'S VERNA GREEN!
HM? IS SHE A FAMOUS ACTOR?

EVEN BETTER! SHE'S A FAMOUS FILM EDITOR!

SHE WORKED ON MY ALL-TIME FAVORITE MOVIE . . . AMERICAN SPRAYPAINT.
HM. I LIKE THAT MOVIE. CAN'T SAY THAT I NOTICED THE EDITING.

EXACTLY.

LOOK! IT'S THE CINEMATOGRAPHER! I HEARD HE'S SHOOTING ON A BANASCOPE 35 . . .
. . . MY DREAM CAMERA.
YOU HAVE DREAMS ABOUT CAMERAS?
IF YOU KNOW ELIJAH, IT'S NOT SURPRISING.

SOUNDS LIKE YOU TWO ARE SPENDING A LOT OF TIME TOGETHER.
NO! I MEAN—
TODAY, YEAH. I WAS SHOWING ELIJAH AROUND THE ISLAND. HE'S MAKING A DOCUMENTARY.

GOOD EVENING, MS. DAGGETT. COULD I INTEREST YOU AND YOUR GUESTS IN A BOWL OF CLAM CHOWDER TO START?

NO, ARTHUR. WE'LL JUMP RIGHT TO THE MAIN COURSE. WHAT'S THE SPECIAL TODAY?

WE HAVE LOBSTER FROM THE NORTH SHORE SERVED WITH A SIDE OF VEGETABLES FROM TISBURY FARM.

SOUNDS YUM! WE'LL TAKE THREE.
RIGHT AWAY, MS. DAGGETT.

SOOO, HOW DID YOU TWO MEET?
KNOCK IT OFF, LEX. WE'RE NOT—
IT'S A FUNNY STORY, ACTUALLY!

GAYLE AND I WENT TO BOSTON ACADEMY TOGETHER!

OH REALLY?
AS THE ACADEMY'S SPORTS DOCUMENTARIAN, I WAS AT ALL HER GAMES.

OH? SO YOU MUST BE A BIG FAN?
YEAH! I MEAN WHO WOULDN'T BE?

BACK AT THE ACADEMY, SHE HAD A 24-1 RECORD, EIGHT NO-HITTERS—

THANKS, ELIJAH. SHE KNOWS.

DID GAYLE TELL YOU — I'M THE CAPTAIN OF HER NEW TEAM, THE VINEYARD BLUEGILLS.
OH! THEN YOU DON'T NEED ME TO TELL YOU HOW GOOD SHE IS!

WELL, IT'S NICE TO BE REMINDED.

YOU MUST BE SO EXCITED TO HAVE A CHAMPIONSHIP PITCHER ON YOUR TEAM.

I WAS. UNTIL I REALIZED OUR CHAMPIONSHIP PITCHER . . .
WASN'T INTERESTED IN BEING JUST A PART OF OUR TEAM.

SHE WANTED TO BE THE WHOLE TEAM.
I NEVER SAID THAT.

ACTIONS SPEAK LOUDER THAN WORDS, TEAMMATE.

YOU TOLD ME YOURSELF, LEX— IT WAS 'CAUSE OF ME THAT THE BLUEGILLS MADE IT TO THEIR FIRST CHAMPIONSHIP GAME.

YEAH, YOU HAD YOUR MOMENT.
THEN YOU HAD TO STEAL MY MOMENT, TOO.

STEAL YOUR MOMENT?!

HA!

HEY, MIZ GREEN.
UH, HOW'S YOUR DINNER?
TRUST ME, YOU DON'T WIN GAMES BY LETTING EVERYONE GET THEIR MOMENT.
I KNOW YOU HEARD ME CALL THE POP-UP.

WE DID TRUST YOU, AND YOU BETRAYED THE TEAM.
I GAVE EVERYTHING I HAD TO THE TEAM.

AND I ENDED UP IN THE EMERGENCY ROOM.

YOU NEVER EVEN CHECKED UP ON ME.

. . .
A TEAM CAPTAIN HAS A LOT OF RESPONSIBILITY.

LOOK AROUND, LEX. YOU HAVE A LOT OF EVERYTHING!

NOW YOU WANT MY APOLOGY, TOO?

GET.

LOST.

WHOA.

WHAT AN EXIT.
HM.

ENJOY.

THIS LOOKS SO DELICIOUS.

BUT I SHOULD CHECK ON GAYLE. SHE'S MY FRIEND.
RIGHT.

CRACK

GAYLE!
WHERE DID YOU GO?

ARE YOU OK?
NEVER MIND, DUMB QUESTION.

I KNOW IT'S NOT REALLY MY BUSINESS . . .
LEX IS A SORE LOSER.
THAT'S ALL YOU NEED TO KNOW.

LIKE THEY SAY, "IT'S JUST A GAME."

A SPORTS SCHOLARSHIP WAS THE ONLY WAY MY MOM COULD AFFORD TUITION AT BOSTON ACADEMY.

I ONLY GOT INTO VINEYARD PREP WITH A LETTER OF RECOMMENDATION FROM MRS. DAGGETT. LEX WANTED ME PLAYING ON HER TEAM.

THE GAME IS MY LIFE.
I'M NOTHING WITHOUT IT.

HEY, STOP THAT. YOU'RE NOT NOTHING.

YOU ARE GAYLE BRIAR.

WITH OR WITHOUT THE GAME.

YOU HAVE A SPECIAL WAY OF SEEING THINGS, ELIJAH. I DON'T THINK I'LL EVER UNDERSTAND IT . . .
BUT I THINK YOU'RE GOING TO BE A GREAT FILMMAKER.

THANKS. THAT MEANS A LOT.
YOU KNOW . . . BACK AT SCHOOL, THE OTHER KIDS THINK I'M JUST SOME NERD OBSESSED WITH CAMERA LENSES AND FILM STOCK.

I THOUGHT THIS SUMMER I COULD COME TO THE ISLAND AND PROVE MYSELF; MAKE A REAL MOVIE AND WIN THE FESTIVAL. SHOW 'EM I'VE GOT SOMETHING TO SAY.

BUT MY SUMMER ENDED BEFORE IT STARTED.

REMEMBER WHEN I SAID MY DAD WASN'T FEELING WELL?
YEAH.

IT'S NOT TRUE.
THIS MORNING I WENT TO WAKE HIM UP, AND HE WAS GONE.

HE FORGOT ALL ABOUT OUR PLAN.
INTERVIEWS ALL DAY. SEE A MOVIE -DAD

WHEN HE'S WORKING ON A STORY, EVERYTHING ELSE JUST DISAPPEARS FOR HIM.

ESPECIALLY ME.
"UNTITLED ISLAND DOCUMENTARY"
★PRODUCTION SCHEDULE★
WEEK ONE
DAY ONE
9AM: TOWN HALL
ISLAND TOUR
W/ GAYLE BRIAR (BRING BIKES)

IT'S ONE DAY, ELIJAH. GIVE HIM A CHANCE. I MEAN, HE BOUGHT YOU ALL THAT STUFF, RIGHT? HE BELIEVES IN YOU!

HE'S ALWAYS BUYING ME STUFF. IT'S HOW HE KEEPS ME DISTRACTED.
ERASE

AND I FALL FOR IT.
EVERY. SINGLE. TIME.
SO YOU'RE JUST GIVING UP ON THE WHOLE THING?

WELL, DUH! YOU CAN'T MAKE A MOVIE ALONE, GAYLE!
HEY, DON'T YELL AT ME. I DIDN'T BAIL ON YOU.

I KNOW. I'M SORRY. I SHOULD HAVE TOLD YOU THIS MORNING. BUT I WANTED TO FEEL LIKE A FILMMAKER FOR A DAY.
GOOD FOR YOU.

AND I KNOW WE HAD A DEAL. I KNOW I PROMISED TO HAVE THE BLACK CAT CREAMERY IN MY MOVIE.

ARE YOU MAD?
NAH, IT DOESN'T MATTER. THERE'S NO CREAMERY TO PROMOTE ANYWAY.
869

WHY NOT?
MONEY'S TIGHT THESE DAYS.
869

I'M SORRY, GAYLE.
YEAH, ME TOO.

I GUESS I'LL SEE YOU AROUND?

WHAT.

THREE THOUSAND DOLLARS?!

GLOBAL STUDIOS PRESENTS:
ISLAND FEST
AUGUST 29th - 31st
CARNIVAL AND
YOUTH FILM FEST
$3,000 IN PRIZES

$3,000?! WHAT KIND OF KIDS' CONTEST GIVES OUT THAT KIND OF MONEY?!

A CONTEST PRESENTED BY GLOBAL STUDIOS.
IT MAKES THEM LOOK GOOD TO SPONSOR A FILM FESTIVAL. IT'S ALL POLITICS.

THREE FREAKING THOUSAND DOLLARS.

HEY . . .
YOU SAID WE MAKE A GOOD TEAM, RIGHT?

YEAH.

WELL, NOW I'VE GOT A PROPOSITION—
YOU AND I MAKE A MOVIE, WIN THE FESTIVAL PRIZE, AND SPLIT THE MONEY.
I PAY BACK MY MOM; YOU IMPRESS YOUR DAD.
EVERYONE WINS.

SHAKE ON IT?

GAYLE BRIAR, DIVISION ONE CHAMPION PITCHER, SMALL-BUSINESS OWNER . . .
AND ASPIRING FILMMAKER.

I KNOW; IMPRESSIVE RIGHT?

YOU KNOW, GAYLE.
THIS ISN'T A PAWNSHOP.

I KNOW, MR. DUKE.
BUT JUST HEAR ME OUT.

I NEED A SMALL LOAN. AS COLLATERAL, I CAN PUT UP MY GLOVE AND MY CLEATS.

GIRL, THAT IS EXACTLY WHAT A PAWNSHOP DOES.
I'M TOO YOUNG TO GO TO A PAWNSHOP! PLEASE, MR. DUKE, I COULD REALLY USE YOUR HELP.

NOW LOOK, I'VE BEEN MORE THAN POLITE ABOUT THE BACK RENT YOUR MOTHER OWES. BUT ASKING FOR A HANDOUT IS A BRIDGE TOO FAR.

I'M NOT ASKING FOR A HANDOUT! I HAVE COLLATERAL.

I KNOW THEY DON'T LOOK LIKE MUCH, BUT THEY'RE VALUABLE TO ME.

I'D LIKE TO TRUST YOU, GAYLE, BUT YOU'RE JUST TOO . . .

UNPREDICTABLE.

I'LL HAVE TO TALK TO YOUR MOTHER.
NO!
SHE CAN'T FIND OUT!

FOR CRYING OUT LOUD, GUS! STOP EMBARRASSING THIS YOUNG LADY! SHE'S NOT A CRIMINAL.

SHE'S TRYING TO TAKE RESPONSIBILITY FOR HERSELF.
I ADMIRE THAT.

NOW, YOU . . .

I'VE BEEN WATCHING YOU BEND OVER BACKWARDS FOR THE HOLLYWOOD FOLKS ALL WEEK. NOW YOU WON'T HELP OUT A FELLOW ISLANDER? RIDICULOUS.

STEP ASIDE, YOU OLD COD.

THANK YOU, MRS. DUKE.
CALL ME MARTHA.

I'LL BE BACK FOR THEM BY THE END OF SUMMER, MARTHA. I PROMISE.
I KNOW. I'LL KEEP 'EM SAFE.

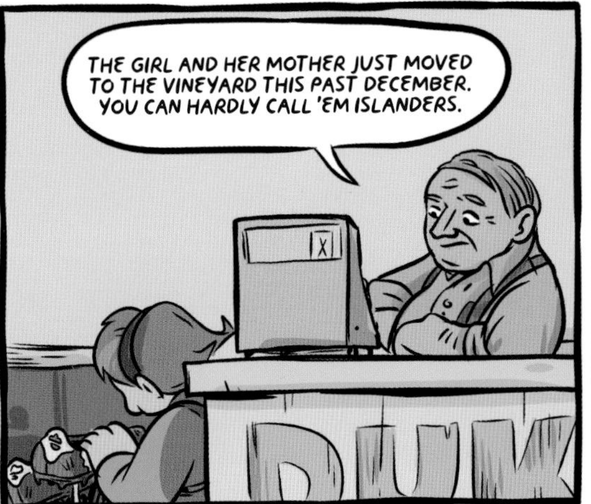
THE GIRL AND HER MOTHER JUST MOVED TO THE VINEYARD THIS PAST DECEMBER. YOU CAN HARDLY CALL 'EM ISLANDERS.

THOSE TWO HAVE BEEN WEATHERING STORMS FROM ALL SIDES SINCE THE DAY THEY ARRIVED, AND THEY HAVEN'T LOST HOPE. IF THAT DOESN'T MAKE THEM ISLANDERS, THEN I DON'T KNOW WHAT DOES.

I'LL NEED A RECEIPT, PLEASE.

HEY!
MOVIE PROP
GUY!

THAT'S ME. WHAT'S
HAPPENING, KID?
YOU HEADING
TO THE WHARF?

SURE AM.
NEED A LIFT?
YEAH!

HOP IN
THE BACK.
WOOO!

AND HANG ON TO
SOMETHING.
QUINT

LET ME GUESS.
ANOTHER PROP?
YUP.
QUINT

BUT ISN'T THE
OCEAN FULL OF
REAL ONES?
NOT MY JOB TO
DEAL WITH REAL.
BESIDES . . .

AMITY
TOWN HALL
CAN'T ALWAYS TRUST REALITY TO ACT THE PART.

GOOD LUCK OUT THERE, KID.
THANK YOU!

GOOD MORNING! I BROUGHT MUFFINS!
FROM THE GRAND ATLANTIC?

YUP! THEY'RE EVEN BETTER THAN THE BISCUITS.
SUMMER SALE

I BROUGHT US SOMETHING, TOO.
OH MY GOSH.
ZODAK VIBRACOLOR. THAT'S EXPENSIVE FILM STOCK!

SUMMER SALE
I KNOW YOUR DAD COULD PROBABLY JUST BUY FILM FOR US, BUT I NEEDED TO DO IT.
I GET THAT, BUT ARE YOU SURE YOU CAN AFFORD ALL THIS?

BLACK CAT CREAMERY
COMING
HONESTLY? NO, I'M NOT SURE. BUT IT'S WORTH THE RISK.

SO TELL ME, MR. DIRECTOR. WHAT IS OUR AWARD-WINNING MOVIE GONNA BE ABOUT?
HUH? I DUNNO.

WHAT DO YOU MEAN "YOU DON'T KNOW"?

I NEVER SAID I WAS A DIRECTOR.
I'M MORE OF A CINEMATOGRAPHER.

STOP TALKING LIKE I KNOW ALL THE WORDS YOU'RE SAYING!
A CINEMATOGRAPHER IS IN CONTROL OF THE CAMERA, BUT—

OUTER HARBOR CRUISES
I NEED A DIRECTOR TO SHOW ME WHERE TO POINT IT!
LIFE JACKETS
WELL, YOU WERE DOING JUST FINE YESTERDAY!

THAT WAS WHEN I HAD A PLAN!
WE DON'T HAVE A PLAN!
WE JUST HAVE FILM AND A CAMERA.

OK, OK. MINOR SETBACK.

SO . . . WE JUST NEED A NEW PLAN, RIGHT?

HOW HARD CAN THAT BE?

HARBOR CRUISES
OK, I'VE GOT A PLAN.
LIFE JACKETS

BABY GOATS.

THAT'S NOT A PLAN, GAYLE.
YES, IT IS! PEOPLE LOVE GOATS! SO, WE MAKE A GOAT MOVIE!

CRUISES
CUTE GOATS DON'T WIN FILM FESTIVALS!
LIFE JACKETS
SO, YOU ADMIT GOATS ARE CUTE!

CRUISES
HA HA HA!
YOU DON'T LOOK LIKE A FILM CREW, BUT YOU SURE CAN ARGUE LIKE ONE.
LIFE JACKETS

IF YOU DON'T MIND ME SAYIN'.

HEY! I KNOW YOU.
YOU'RE CHARLIE POTTER!

OH MIGHTY, KID.
FORTY YEARS IN THE MOVIE BIZ AND NO ONE HAS EVER RECOGNIZED ME IN PUBLIC.

CHARLIE WHO?

CHARLIE POTTER!

MOVIE FX MAGAZINE'S "WIZARD OF THE YEAR" THREE YEARS IN A ROW.
WAS IT THREE?

HE'S A MASTER OF CREATURE EFFECTS!
THEY CALL HIM "KING OF THE MONSTERS!"

ROAR!

HE'S FAMOUS!
I'M NOT SURE YOU KNOW WHAT "FAMOUS" MEANS.

"FAMOUS" IS A STRETCH.
I DO PREFER TO STAY BEHIND THE SCENES.
DON'T BE MODEST. YOU MADE SOME OF THE MOST ICONIC MONSTERS IN MOVIE HISTORY!

THE SPACE BAT FROM INTERGALACTIC MEGA KNIGHT!

THE GIANT SQUID IN
SEVEN SEAS OF JUPITER!

THE CYBER SPHINX IN
FUTURE PHARAOH 3000!

FOG
FROG!

YOU'VE ACTUALLY SEEN FOG FROG?
IT'S TERRIFYING! I LOVE IT!

GAYLE, YOU GOTTA WATCH FOG FROG.
I DON'T DO HORROR MOVIES.

THEY AIN'T SCARY WHEN YOU'RE BEHIND THE CAMERA.
JUST A LOT OF RUBBER AND PAINT.

BOY, I WISH I HAD YOUR IMAGINATION.
YEAH, IT PAYS THE BILLS.

BUT I'M MORE INTERESTED IN WHAT THE YOUNG FOLKS ARE MAKING. I ASSUME Y'ALL KNOW ABOUT THE FILM FESTIVAL? BIG PRIZE MONEY.
YEAH, WE KNOW.

MIND IF I ASK WHAT YOUR FILM IS ABOUT?
HMMM. IT'S KINDA HARD TO EXPLAIN.
ISLAND FEST

DON'T WORRY ABOUT IT. SOMETIMES A MOVIE DOESN'T TAKE SHAPE UNTIL THE EDITING ROOM.
SNIP SNIP
THAT'S GOOD TO KNOW.

BUT YOU MUST HAVE A STORY YOU'RE WORKING FROM?
WELL, I CAN SHOW YOU WHAT WE DO HAVE.

DID YOU SEE THE GOATS?

IF YOU DON'T MIND ME SAYING . . . YOU TWO COULD USE INSPIRATION.
I GOT A THOUGHT — HOW 'BOUT I SHOW YOU MY WORKSHOP?

THAT'S A "YES, PLEASE."

HEY YA, CARL.
I WANNA SHOW THESE YOUNG FILMMAKERS THE WORKSHOP.
NO PROBLEM.

BUT THAT CAMERA'S GOTTA STAY WITH ME. SORRY, KID. NO PICTURES.
OH. OK.

WHY NO PICTURES, CHARLIE?
STUDIO RULES. WE CAN'T HAVE OUR SECRETS LEAKING TO THE PRESS. THAT'D SPOIL THE SURPRISE!

SURPRISE?

NOW, I GOT ONE RULE— DON'T TOUCH ANYTHING WITH TEETH.

HA HA! HE'S KIDDING.
I THINK.

WELCOME TO SHARK CITY.
ORCA

LOUISIANA
SCUBA

HEY, CHARLIE!
CAN I HAVE ONE OF THESE SHIRTS?
NOPE. CREW MEMBERS ONLY.
SHARK

EFFECTS
EFFECTS

WOW! IS THIS A REAL HARPOON GUN?!
NOPE.
PROPERTY OF GLOBAL STUDIOS

DOES IT SHOOT?!
IT'S A PROP, ELIJAH.

WHOA . . . IS THIS FAKE BLOOD IN HERE? CAN I HAVE SOME?
WHY NOT? GRAB A CUP.
FAST DRY

IT'S SO STICKY! WHAT'S IN IT?
CORN SYRUP AND FOOD COLORING.

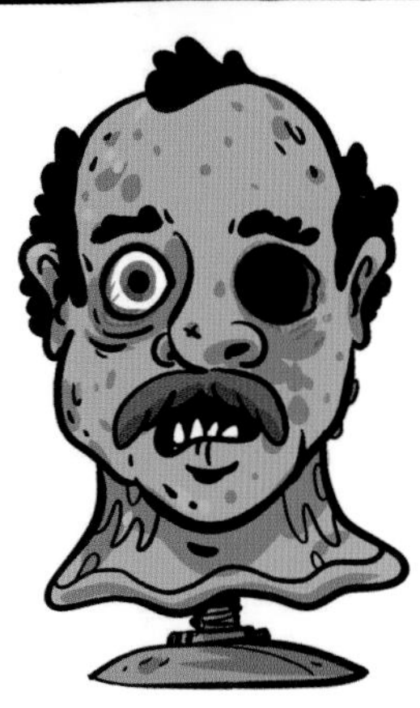

SO YOU CAN EAT IT?
WELL, IT IS A LAXATIVE.
CLICK

WHA
A LAXA
VRRR

RRRRRR
WHAT?! WHAT DID I DO?

RRRRRRR
SWITCH? WHAT SWITCH?!

RRRRRR
AH.

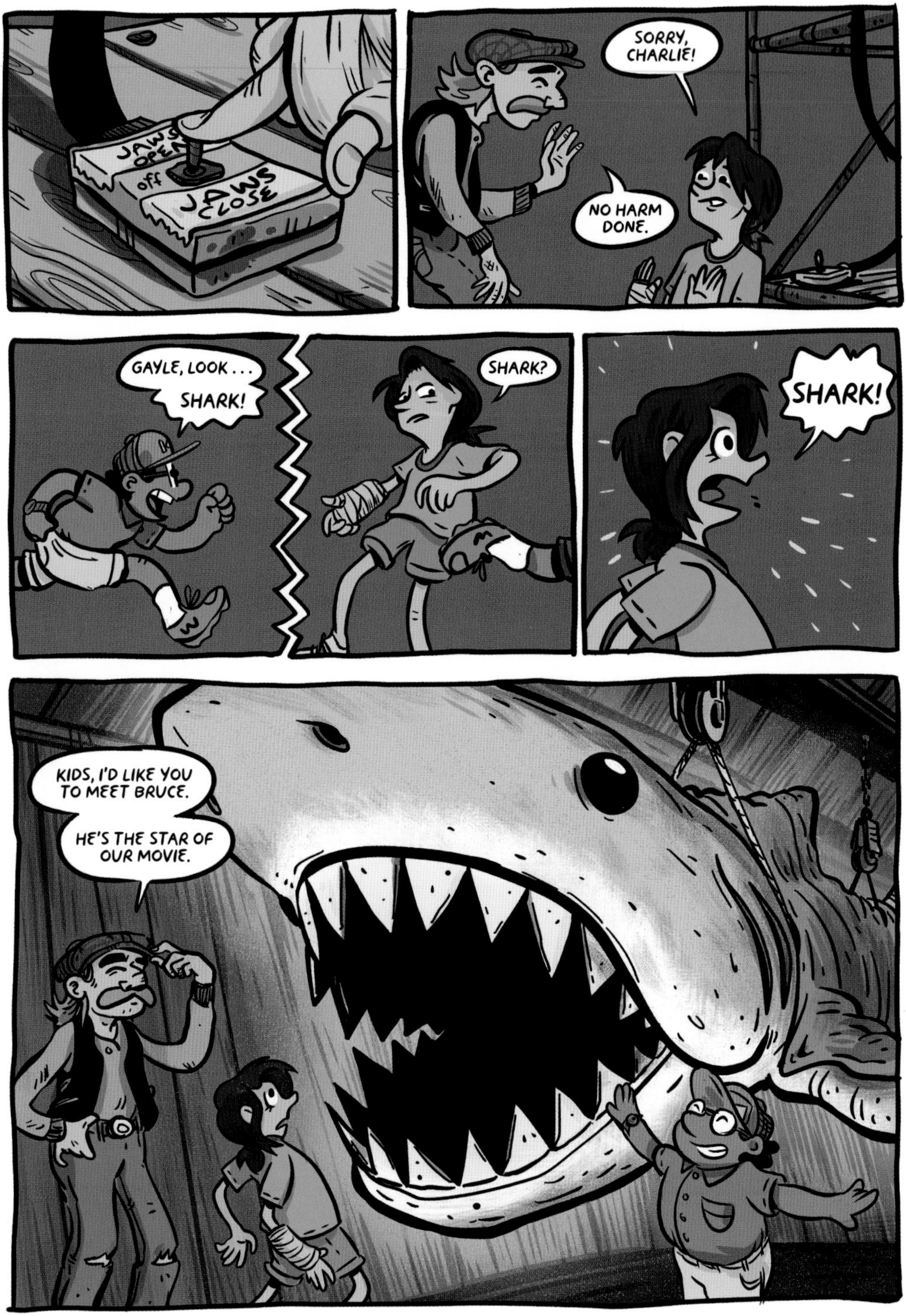

KIDS, I'D LIKE YOU TO MEET BRUCE.

HE'S THE STAR OF OUR MOVIE.

CHARLIE, YOU'RE A MAGICIAN! YOU GOTTA HELP US WITH OUR MOVIE.

AH, I DON'T KNOW, I HAVE A LOT ON MY PLATE. OL' BRUCE AIN'T EVEN WATERWORTHY YET.

COME ON, CHARLIE! HELP US WIN THE FILM FESTIVAL!

LOOK, I'M JUST AN EFFECTS MAN. I CAN BUILD A SHARK, BUT I CAN'T BRING HIM TO LIFE, YOU GET ME?
BRUCE LOOKS REAL ENOUGH TO ME.

IT AIN'T ABOUT THE SHARK. IT'S ABOUT THE STORY. THE STORY IS WHERE THE REAL MAGIC COMES FROM.
BUT WE DON'T HAVE A STORY!

WHEN I READ THE SCRIPT FOR THIS MOVIE, I KNEW IT WAS SOMETHING I WANTED TO BE A PART OF.
THE STORY IS WHY I'M HERE. IT'S WHY WE'RE ALL HERE. IT'S EVERYTHING.
SHARK!

YOU WANNA STAND A CHANCE AT WINNING THAT FILM FESTIVAL?
FIND A STORY WORTH TELLING AND THE REST WILL FALL INTO PLACE.

"THE SHELL FISHERMEN OF MENEMSHA POND CARRY STORIES OF THE ISLAND IN THEIR BLOOD AND BONES."

THAT'S WHAT MY DAD SAYS, ANYWAY. IF THERE'S A STORY WORTH TELLING, WE'LL FIND IT THERE.

SO, WHERE DO WE START?
HM . . .
LET'S TALK TO THAT GUY. HE LOOKS LIKE HE'S GOT SOME STORIES.

HELLO, SIR? UH, MY NAME IS GAYLE, AND THIS IS ELIJAH. WE'RE MAKING A FILM ABOUT THE ISLAND.
DO YOU HAVE A FEW MINUTES TO TALK TO US?

YOU FROM HOLLYWOOD?
NO, SIR. I LIVE HERE.

THEY'VE BEEN COMING ROUND LOOKING FOR "REAL" ISLANDERS TO PUT IN THEIR MOVIE.
BUT NOT ME.

I WAS A BIT TOO REAL FOR THEM.

WE'RE NOT LOOKING FOR ACTORS. WE'RE LOOKING FOR A STORY.
I'M A FOURTH-GENERATION ISLANDER. I'VE GOT MORE TALES THAN A SCHOOL OF TUNA.

TUNA TALES. AMAZING.
COULD YOU SAY THAT AGAIN FOR THE CAMERA?

THIS STORY AIN'T FREE, KID.

HEY, I BOUGHT THE FILM.

LET'S SEE, I'VE GOT—
HEY!
THAT'LL DO.

GATHER ROUND
AND LISTEN WELL!

TO A TALE I'VE
LONGED TO TELL!

THE STORY OF OLD
GRANDPA LESTER . . .

WHO ONCE FOUGHT
THE GOOSE FROM HELL.

. . . AS GRAN'PA ROWED CLOSER, HE COULD SEE THE COLD FIRES OF HELL RAGING BEHIND THE MONSTER'S BEADY EYES.
MAYBE YOU SHOULD OFFER HIM MORE MONEY.

HEY, DO YOU HEAR THAT?
IT'S A POLICE CHASE!

AND WHAT THE HECK IS THAT?

LOOKS LIKE A . . .

CAPTAIN?

OOP!

OH MY GOSH, IT'S GHASTLY MADDIE.
THE GIRL IN THE LIGHTHOUSE?

HALT! IN THE NAME OF THE LAW.

ELIJAH, WHAT ARE YOU DOING?
YOU SAID SHE'S AN INTERESTING LANDMARK. WE SHOULD TALK TO HER.

SURE, WE CAN GO VISIT HER IN JAIL.
HEY, WANT TO MAKE ANOTHER FEW DOLLARS?

UFF HUFF HUFF HUFF HUFF HUFF

AFTERNOON, CHIEF. HAVEN'T SEEN YOU ROUND THE POND LATELY.

WHERE'D THEY GO, SHELLY?
WHERE DID WHO GO?

THE CAPTAIN.

AS YOU CAN SEE I'M MENDING TRAPS WITH MY. . . NIECE.
THAT'S ME!

WE HAVEN'T SEEN ANY CAPTAINS. BESIDES ME, OF COURSE.
WANNA CHECK MY SHACK?
SHELLY

NOW, SHELLY, YOU WOULDN'T BE SENDING ME ON A WILD-GOOSE CHASE, WOULD YOU?
YOU KNOW I AIN'T NO FRIEND TO GEESE, CHIEF.

ALL I KNOW IS . . . A MYSTERIOUS HOOLIGAN HAS BEEN HARASSING THE HOLLYWOOD FOLKS AND IT'S PUTTING THEM BEHIND SCHEDULE.

THE SHARK MOVIE IS GOOD FOR THE ISLAND AND WE WANT TO KEEP THOSE MOVIE FOLKS HAPPY.
YOU GOT IT, CHIEF.

KEEP AN EYE OUT FOR TROUBLE. WE GOT A LONG SUMMER AHEAD.

HOLD ON!
WE JUST WANT TO
TALK TO YOU.

LET HER GO, ELIJAH.
SHE'S A CRAZY WEIRDO
VAMPIRE GIRL.

I HEARD THAT SHE
BELIEVES IN GHOSTS.

I BELIEVE IN EVIL.
THERE'S A DIFFERENCE.

WHAT'S WITH
THE COSTUME?
I WAS TRYING TO
GET THE ATTENTION OF
THE FILMMAKERS.

LET THEM KNOW THIS ISLAND HAS ITS OWN SHARK STORY;
THE ONLY ONE WORTH TELLING.

SO YOU'VE GOT A STORY WORTH TELLING, HUH?

YEAH.
WITH A *REAL* MONSTER SHARK. MUCH SCARIER THAN ANYTHING HOLLYWOOD COULD DREAM UP.

OK, SO YOU DON'T BELIEVE IN GHOSTS, BUT YOU BELIEVE IN SEA MONSTERS.

YOU'VE BEEN STUCK ON THIS ISLAND TOO LONG. LET'S GO, ELIJAH.
HOLD ON, I WANT TO HEAR HER STORY.
IT'S NOT A STORY. IT'S THE TRUTH. THEY CALL IT —

THE ATWOOD TERROR.

THE ATWOOD TERROR?

THE ATWOOD TERROR.

I THINK I KNOW THAT ONE . . .
WE CALLED IT "GHOST SHARK."

YEAH, IT'S TOLD AT EVERY SLEEPOVER IN MASSACHUSETTS. IT'S DUMB, AND IT'S NOT SCARY.

IF YOU'RE NOT SCARED, YOU DON'T KNOW THE REAL STORY.

THEN WHY DON'T YOU TELL IT TO US?

WHAT, REALLY?
YEAH. WE WANNA HEAR IT.

DON'T WE, GAYLE?

FINE.

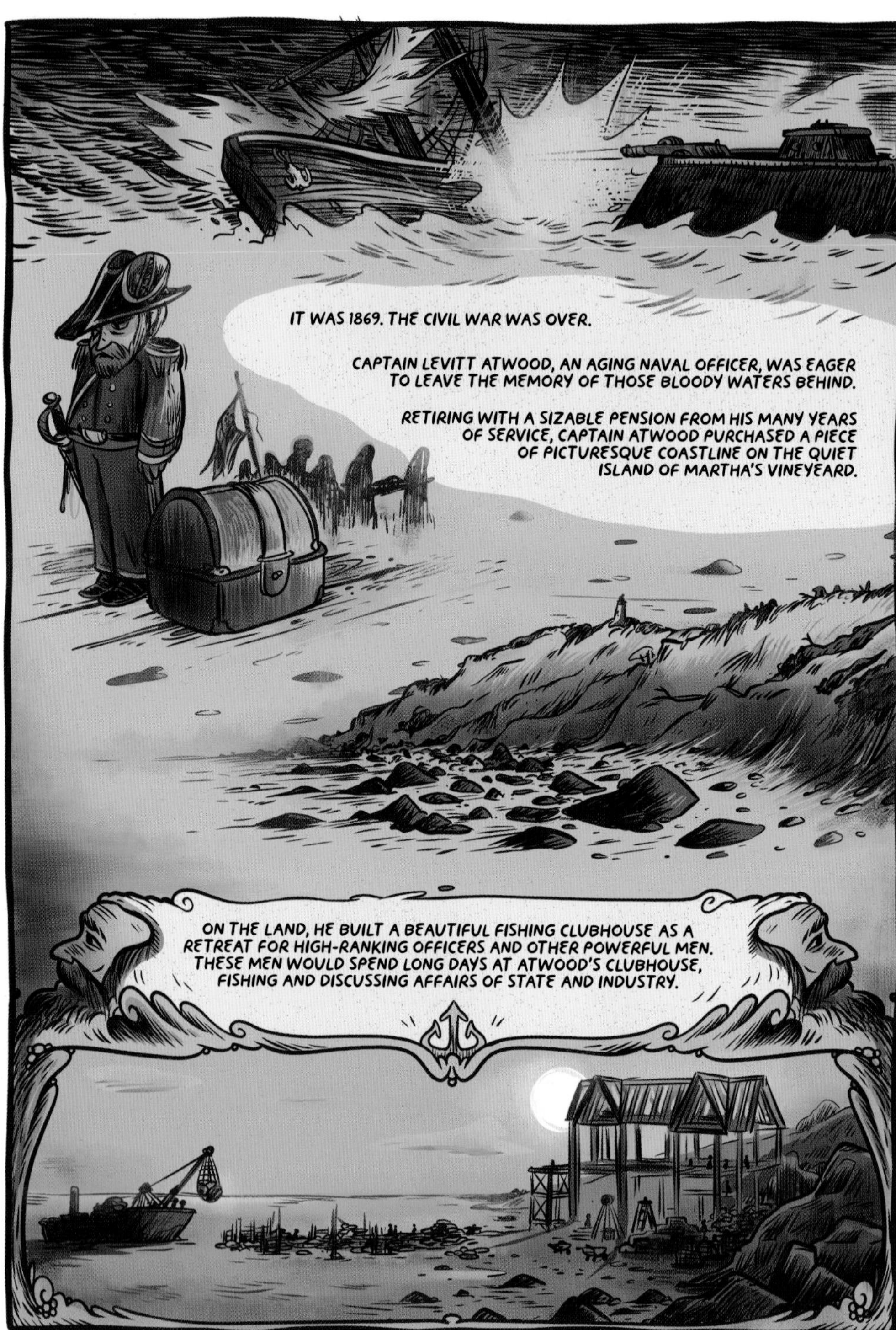
IT WAS 1869. THE CIVIL WAR WAS OVER.
CAPTAIN LEVITT ATWOOD, AN AGING NAVAL OFFICER, WAS EAGER TO LEAVE THE MEMORY OF THOSE BLOODY WATERS BEHIND.
RETIRING WITH A SIZABLE PENSION FROM HIS MANY YEARS OF SERVICE, CAPTAIN ATWOOD PURCHASED A PIECE OF PICTURESQUE COASTLINE ON THE QUIET ISLAND OF MARTHA'S VINEYEARD.
ON THE LAND, HE BUILT A BEAUTIFUL FISHING CLUBHOUSE AS A RETREAT FOR HIGH-RANKING OFFICERS AND OTHER POWERFUL MEN. THESE MEN WOULD SPEND LONG DAYS AT ATWOOD'S CLUBHOUSE, FISHING AND DISCUSSING AFFAIRS OF STATE AND INDUSTRY.

THE CULMINATION OF POWER AT SUCH A REMOTE LOCATION BEGAN TO LURE UNDERWORLD CRIMINALS, AND IT WASN'T LONG UNTIL THE CLUBHOUSE WAS A SANCTUM OF SHADY FIGURES.
PLAYING HOST TO VILLAINOUS MEN REQUIRES A QUIET DISPOSITION.
AND FOR HIS DISCRETION, THE CAPTAIN WAS REWARDED WITH RESPECT AND RICHES.
BUT THESE VILLAINS DID NOT MAKE HIS LIFE EASY.
THE APPETITES OF CORRUPT MEN ARE NEVER SATISFIED, AND THEY GREW TIRED OF PIER FISHING AND THE LEISURE ACTIVITIES OF COMMON PEOPLE.
THE CAPTAIN STRUGGLED TO KEEP THE DEVILS HAPPY.

ONE NIGHT, CAPTAIN ATWOOD DISCOVERED A DEAD MAN WITH A KNIFE IN HIS BACK HIDDEN UNDER A BED.
THE RESULT OF A DEAL GONE BAD.
WISHING TO AVOID THE ATTENTION OF THE LAW, THE CAPTAIN CHOPPED UP THE BODY AND DISPOSED OF IT OFF THE END OF HIS PIER.
WATCHING A DEAD BODY SINK WOULD HAVE BEEN ENOUGH TO CHANGE A PERSON FOR LIFE.
BUT ATWOOD HAD WATCHED MANY BODIES SINK DURING HIS TIME AT WAR. ANOTHER ONE MADE NO DIFFERENCE.

CAPTAIN ATWOOD AWOKE THE NEXT MORNING TO FIND HIS GUESTS CROWDED ALONG THE PIER, CHEERING ALONG AS A TIGER SHARK FED ON THE SCRAPS OF FRESH HUMAN FLESH.
BELIEVING THE BLOODY SCENE HAD BEEN STAGED FOR THEIR ENJOYMENT, THEY COMMENDED THE CAPTAIN.
RELIEF SWEPT OVER HIM. HE WAS SAVED BY THE SEA.
THE CAPTAIN HAD SPENT HIS LIFE SERVING THE SEA AND BELIEVED THE SHARK TO BE A GIFT FROM THE GOD POSEIDON HIMSELF.
AS A HOST TO CRIMINAL SCUM, THE CAPTAIN HAD NO TROUBLE FINDING MORE BODIES.
WITHIN DAYS, A FRENZY OF SHARKS CIRCLED BELOW HIS PIER; ONLY THEIR FINS WERE VISIBLE IN THE CLOUDY, RED WATER.

ON A HOT SUMMER NIGHT, A NEW GUEST ARRIVED AT HIS MIDNIGHT OFFERING:
A GREAT WHITE SHARK.
THE GIANT BEGAN TO DEVOUR THE LESSER SHARKS UNTIL IT ALONE RULED THE WATERS BELOW THE CAPTAIN'S JETTY.
WORD OF CAPTAIN ATWOOD'S GREAT WHITE SPREAD QUICKLY, AND MANY WHO CAME PAID TRIBUTE WITH GLORIOUS RICHES.
BUT THE GREATEST REWARD WAS THE COMPANY OF THE SHARK ITSELF.
THE OLD SOLDIER FOUND KINSHIP IN THE MONSTER'S COLD, BLACK EYES.

HE BEGAN TO DRESS IN A DEEP GRAY CLOAK AND HUNG A TALISMAN AROUND HIS NECK, A TRIBUTE TO THE MIGHTY SEA GOD.
ATWOOD'S OFFERINGS TO THE GREAT WHITE EVOLVED INTO AN ELABORATE RITUAL.
THOSE WHO GATHERED WERE DUBBED "THE FOLLOWERS OF THE BLACK EYE."
BUT IT WAS NOT TO LAST. WITHOUT RHYME OR REASON, THE GREAT WHITE DISAPPEARED.

THE SPECTACLE WAS GONE, AND THE GUESTS QUICKLY GREW BORED WITH THE CAPTAIN'S CULTISH RAMBLINGS.
BY THE END OF SUMMER, THE ROOMS OF THE ATWOOD CLUBHOUSE WERE ALL VACANT.
WITHOUT THE PROTECTION OF THE CRIME BOSSES, CAPTAIN ATWOOD KNEW IT WOULDN'T BE TOO LONG BEFORE THE LAW OF THE LAND CAST JUDGMENT ON HIM.
THE CAPTAIN LOCKED HIMSELF IN HIS ROOM, GROWING MORE PARANOID BY THE DAY.

ONE NIGHT IN THE LAST DAYS OF SUMMER, HE AWOKE TO THE SOUND OF A RAGING STORM KNOCKING AT THE DOORS OF HIS CLUBHOUSE.
CAPTAIN ATWOOD DONNED HIS CEREMONIAL CLOAK AND WENT TO THE END OF THE JETTY.
HE CURSED THE SEA GOD WHO HAD ABANDONED HIM.
AS IF IN RESPONSE, A PHANTOM SHARK ROSE UP FROM THE WATER.
THE MONSTER CAUGHT CAPTAIN ATWOOD IN ITS JAWS AND DRAGGED HIS BODY BELOW THE WAVES.

YOU HAVE A WAY WITH WORDS, GHASTLY MADDIE.

PLEASE STOP CALLING ME THAT.

IF THE CAPTAIN IS DEAD, WHO TOLD HIS STORY?

SOME STORIES JUST FIND THEIR WAY.

OK, I GUESS.
BUT HIS CLUBHOUSE MUST BE ON A MAP—
I HAVEN'T FOUND IT YET.

MAYBE BECAUSE IT DOESN'T EXIST.

THERE'S MORE THAN ONE MAP OF THE ISLAND.

FORGET THIS. I DON'T HAVE TO EXPLAIN MYSELF TO SOME KIDS.

WAIT, MADDIE!
WE BELIEVE YOU!

WE WHAT?
MURDER, CULTS, AND SEA MONSTERS.

COME ON, GAYLE, THIS IS THE PERFECT STORY FOR A MOVIE.

IT IS CREEPY. I'LL GIVE YOU THAT.

THEN YOU'LL HELP ME REACH THE FILMMAKERS?

WE HEARD THE CHIEF; THEY WON'T HAVE ANYTHING TO DO WITH YOU. THAT'S NOT HOW YOUR STORY IS GOING TO GET TOLD.

GET TO THE POINT, KID.

THEY'RE NOT THE ONLY ONES ON THIS ISLAND WITH A FILM CAMERA.
YOU'RE KIDDING.

HEY, YOU SAID YOU LIKED HER STORY.
I SAID IT WAS CREEPY.

WHAT THE HECK ARE YOU TWO TALKING ABOUT?!

MAYBE WE CAN HELP EACH OTHER OUT.

GAYLE...

WE HAVE A PROPOSITION FOR YOU.
WHAT KIND OF PROPOSITION?
SAVE ME.

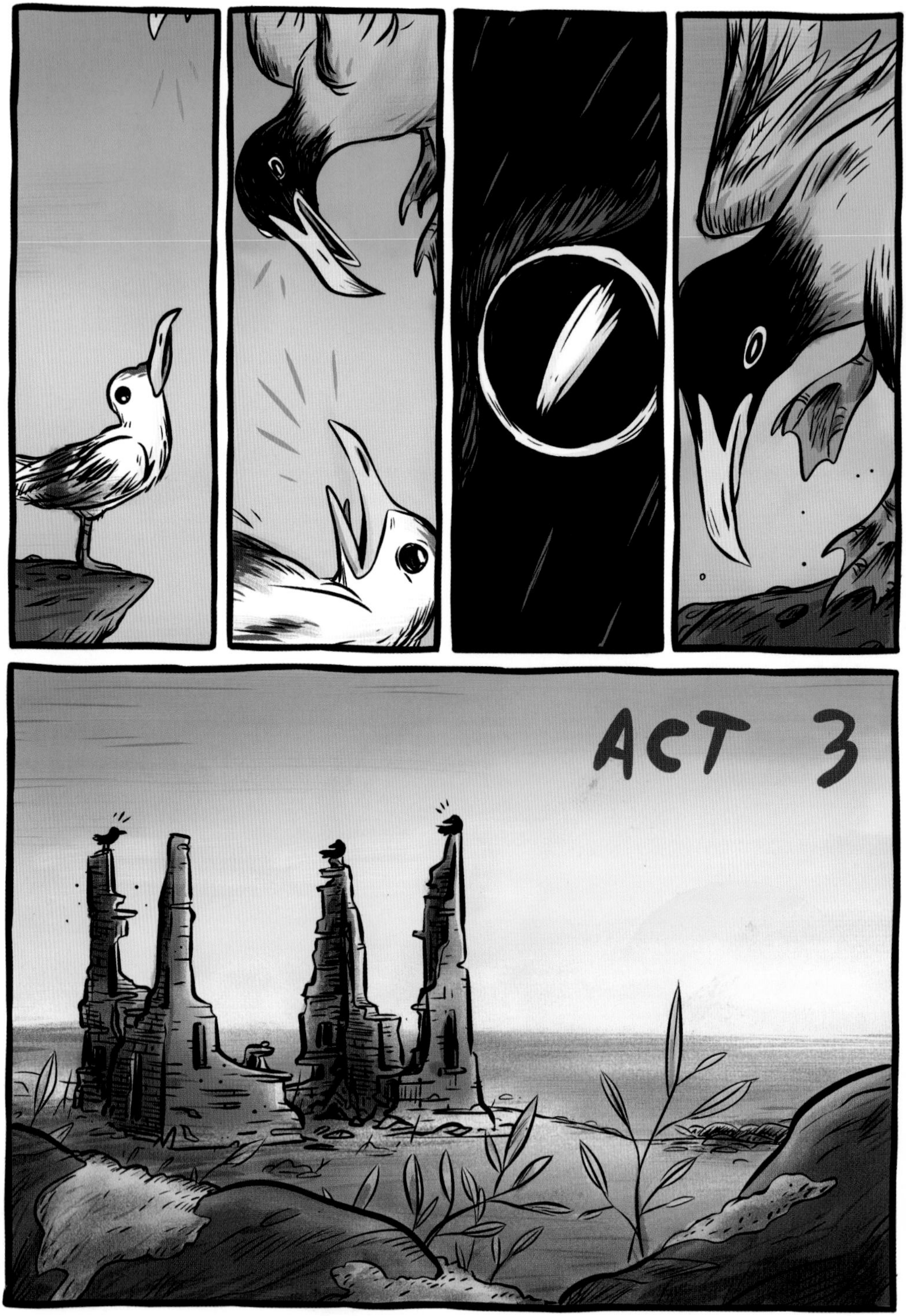

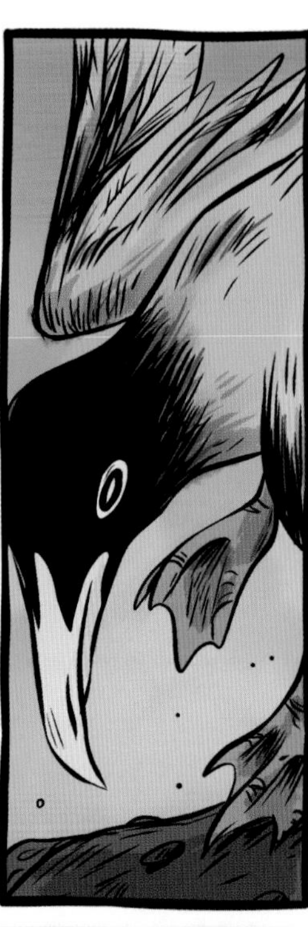

ACT 3

THE DEAD HAVE RISEN!

MORNING, SLEEPYHEAD.

YOUR FRIEND MADISON IS HERE.
I SEE THAT.

WE SAID WE WERE GOING TO MEET AT THE WHARF.

I WOKE UP EARLY. I THOUGHT WE'D WALK OVER TOGETHER.

TIME FOR BREAKFAST, SMUDGE.

MADISON WAS TELLING ME ABOUT YOUR MOVIE! THAT'S SO EXCITING!
YEAH.
SMUDGE

THE ATWOOD TERROR . . . OH MY GOSH. MY FRIENDS AND I USED TO SCARE EACH OTHER SILLY TALKING ABOUT THAT PHANTOM SHARK.

WE WERE AFRAID TO GO IN THE WATER!

BUT I LIKE THE WAY YOU TELL IT, MADISON. THERE'S A BIT MORE TO IT.

THAT'S SO FLATTERING, MS. BRIAR. THANK YOU.
MY PARENTS STUDY LOCAL HISTORY, SO I KNOW LOTS OF THE OLD STORIES.

MROW.
SHUT UP, SMUDGE.
SMUDGE

CAN I HELP?
I GOT IT.
GOODNESS' SAKE, GAYLE. DON'T BE SO PROUD.

I THINK IT'S WONDERFUL YOU FOUND EACH OTHER. GAYLE HAS BEEN MOPING AROUND THE HOUSE SINCE HER LAST GAME—
OOPS, IT'S TIME TO GO!
SMUDGE

I'M JUST SAYING! IT'S GOOD TO TRY NEW THINGS.
THANKS FOR THE COFFEE, MS. BRIAR.

I'M WORKING A DOUBLE, SO I'LL BE HOME LATE. LOVE YOU!

I KNOW! LOVE YOU!

WHY ARE YOU HERE, MADDIE?
I THOUGHT YOU AND I SHOULD TALK.
SHARK!

FINE, LET'S TALK.
I KNOW KIDS TALK. I DON'T CARE WHAT YOU'VE HEARD ABOUT ME, AND I DON'T WANT IT TO GET IN THE WAY.

I NEED TO TELL THIS STORY.

AND I NEED TO WIN THAT PRIZE MONEY.

GAMBLING DEBT?
HOSPITAL BILL.

I'M THE REASON SHE WORKS DOUBLE SHIFTS.

BUT IF SHE FINDS OUT I'M DOING THIS FOR HER—
RELAX, I CAN KEEP A SECRET.

JUST DO THIS THING MY WAY AND I'LL GET YOU THAT MONEY.
DEAL.

ISLAND FEST
AUGUST 29th - 31st
FUNNY. I THOUGHT THERE'D BE A LOT MORE ARGUING ON THIS WALK.
YEAH, ME TOO.

PLEASED TO MEET YOU, MADDIE. SO THIS IS YOUR STORY, HUH?
IT IS.

IT'S DARN GOOD.
I KNOW.

I'M SORRY, WHAT ARE WE DOING HERE?

WHY DON'T Y'ALL PULL UP A BARREL AND FIND OUT?

SO, YOU'VE GOT YOURSELVES A STORY TO TELL. NOW THE QUESTION IS . . .
HOW DO YOU TELL IT?

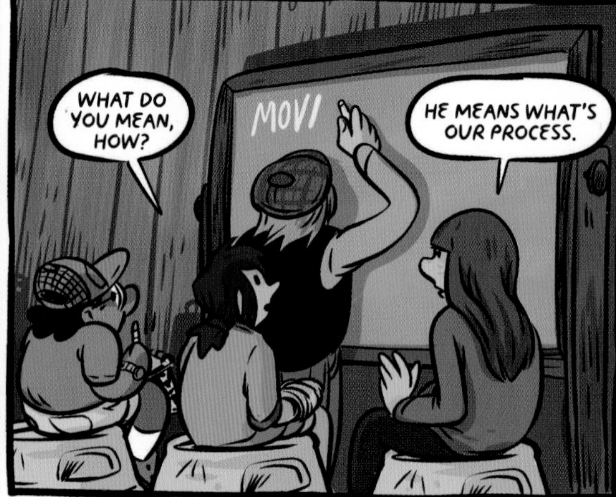
MOVI
WHAT DO YOU MEAN, HOW?
HE MEANS WHAT'S OUR PROCESS.

WE LET IT EVOLVE NATURALLY. NO GIMMICKS. NO SPECIAL EFFECTS.

ATWOOD'S SPIRIT LOOMS OVER THE WHOLE ISLAND. IF WE LOOK CLOSE ENOUGH, THE TRUTH WILL REVEAL ITSELF.
WHAT?
I DO HAVE A ZOOM LENS.

THAT'S A BEAUTIFUL SENTIMENT, MADDIE. VERY POETIC.

BUT MOVIEMAKING ISN'T ABOUT POETRY.

MOVIEMAKING IS ABOUT STRUCTURE.

THE FESTIVAL DEADLINE IS AUGUST 29TH AT SUNDOWN. SIX WEEKS FROM TODAY.

WHICH MEANS YOUR WHOLE PROCESS NEEDS TO FIT IN HERE.
MOVIE MAKING 101
1 2 3 4 5 6

LET'S START WITH ASSIGNING EACH WEEK A BASIC TASK.

TELL ME . . .
WHAT DO YOU NEED TO MAKE YOUR MOVIE?
MOVIE MAKING 101
1 2 3 4 5 6

WE NEED FOOTAGE.
OF WHAT?

FOOTAGE OF ANSWERS.
FROM WHO?

ANSWERS FROM . . . ISLANDERS?
I LIKE IT!

EXCUSE ME, MISS:
DO YOU BELIEVE IN PHANTOM SHARKS?
HA!

SO WE START BY INTERVIEWING ISLANDERS ABOUT THE ATWOOD TERROR.
LET'S SAY THAT'S WEEK ONE.
MOVIE M
1 2

BUT WE NEED MORE THAN TALKING HEADS ON THE SCREEN.

YEAH, WE NEED B-ROLL!

DON'T JUST TELL. SHOW YOUR STORY.
THAT'S WEEK TWO.
IE MAKI
2

ONCE WE HAVE OUR FOOTAGE, HOW DO WE PUT IT TOGETHER?

LEAVE THAT TO ME. MY DAD'LL GET ME AN EDITING MACHINE.

WHAT ARE YOU, RICH?
NOT RICH. JUST SPOILED.
THAT'S WEEK THREE, CHARLIE.

MOVIE MAKI
1 2 3
ACCORDING TO THE CHART, WE'VE GOT TIME TO SPARE!

YOU'VE GOT TO ACCOUNT FOR A FEW VARIABLES.
LIKE WHAT?

BAD WEATHER

BLURRY FOOTAGE

GARBLED AUDIO

DEAD BATTERIES

RUINED PLANS

WASTED TIME

BURNING MONEY

LOUSY MOODS

MOVIE MAKING 101
1 2 3 4 5 6
NOW, THAT'S WHAT MOVIEMAKING IS REALLY LIKE.

THAT'S PRETTY MUCH MY LIFE ALREADY.
HM.
BUT THE DEADLINE! HOW WILL WE GET IT DONE IN TIME?

THE ONLY WAY ANYTHING GETS DONE: YOU LEARN TO WORK TOGETHER.

THAT MEANS EVERYONE DOES THEIR JOB.

MADDIE—YOU'RE THE DIRECTOR.

BELIEVE IN THE STORY AND FOLLOW IT NO MATTER WHAT.

FOLLOW THE STORY.

ELIJAH—YOU'RE THE CAMERAMAN.

KEEP THE CAMERA ROLLING AND CAPTURE EVERYTHING.

CAPTURE EVERYTHING.

GAYLE—YOU'RE THE ON-SCREEN PRESENCE.
THE WHAT?

HE MEANS YOU'RE GOING TO BE IN THE MOVIE.

BUT I'M NOT AN ACTOR!

YOU'RE THE INTERVIEWER IN A DOCUMENTARY. SO JUST ACT NATURAL.

MAKE MADDIE DO IT! IT'S HER STORY.

YOU'RE BETTER AT ASKING RIDICULOUS QUESTIONS.
WHAT'S THAT SUPPOSED TO MEAN?

COME ON, GAYLE, MADDIE AND I DON'T BELONG IN FRONT OF A CAMERA.

AT LEAST YOU'RE USED TO THE SPOTLIGHT.

WE NEED YOU OUT THERE.
OK.

HM, WELL . . .
YOU STILL DON'T LOOK MUCH LIKE A FILM CREW.

THEN IT'S A GOOD THING WE HAVE YOU, CHARLIE!
SPORTSMEN'S PARADISE
007o981
'72 LOUISIANA
WELL, THE THING ABOUT THAT IS . . .

BRUCE IS KEEPING ME PRETTY BUSY.

OH.
DON'T SOUND SO GLUM. YOU'LL BE FINE. BETTER THAN FINE, EVEN!
PROPERTY OF GLOBAL STUDIOS

'CAUSE I'M GONNA GIVE YOU THE ONE THING EVERY REAL FILM CREW NEEDS.

A LEG?

NO, ELIJAH. NOT A LEG.
WHAT IS IT?

OH MY GOSH. IT'S . . .
BEAUTIFUL.

GLOBAL city STUDIOS
02074
PROD Atwood Terror
DIR M. Grey
CAM E. Jones
Day 1 | take 1

THIS IS MARTHA'S VINEYARD.

AN ISLAND OF ENDLESS BEACHES.

STUNNING LANDSCAPES.

AND NATURAL BEAUTY.
SLOW

THE WAMPANOAG NAMED IT "NOEPE."

EXCUSE ME, THIS IS A LIBRARY. YOU CAN'T—
SHH!
WHICH MEANS: IN THE MIDST OF THE SEA.

AS THE NAME SUGGESTS, THE ISLAND FEELS FAR REMOVED FROM THE HUSTLE AND BUSTLE OF THE MAINLAND.

WHICH IS WHY SO MANY HAVE COME HERE TO RECONNECT WITH THE NATURAL WORLD.

THOSE LOOKING FOR TRADITION . . .
THOSE LOOKING FOR INSPIRATION . . .
THOSE LOOKING FOR ANSWERS . . .

MOST OF THEIR NAMES ARE FORGOTTEN,
LIKE FOOTPRINTS IN THE SAND.

BUT ONE NAME REFUSES TO FADE AWAY.

CUT.

HOW WAS THAT, MADDIE?

YOU KNOW WHAT, GAYLE? IT WAS PRETTY GOOD.
THAT'S IT! OUR FIRST DAY IS A WRAP!
WOO!

HEY, KIDDO, HOW WAS YOUR FIRST DAY AS A MOVIE STAR?
AWESOME. HOW ARE YOU?

I'M BURNT OUT.
ARE YOU WEARING MY OLD BLAZER?
YUP!

WHAT ARE YOU WATCHING?
KING KONG.

I'M GOING UPSTAIRS TO LEARN MY LINES FOR TOMORROW.
WAIT, WAIT, THIS IS THE BEST SCENE! COME HERE!

THIS IS SO DUMB.

I MEAN, WHY WOULD SHE GO SOMEWHERE CALLED "SKULL ISLAND" IN THE FIRST PLACE?!

DOES SHE WANT TO GET EATEN BY A GIANT APE?!
SHE'S A STRUGGLING ACTOR.

SEE THAT GUY? HE'S THE DESPERATE DIRECTOR WHO PROMISED HER THE STAR ROLE IN HIS NEW MOVIE.

DOCK ST. COFFEE SHOP
OPEN
OH MAN, MY MOM USED TO TELL ME AN' MY BROTHER THAT ATWOOD STORY ALL THE TIME!

SHE'D SAY IF WE WENT SWIMMING AFTER DARK THE PHANTOM SHARK WOULD EAT US.

JUST LIKE IT ATE THAT OLD ARMY GUY.

ACTUALLY, HE WAS A NAVAL OFFICER.
QUIET, MADDIE.

DO YOU BELIEVE THE STORY?
ME? NAH.

BUT THIS PLACE IS SO BORING, YOU KNOW?
I COULD SEE HOW SOMEONE MIGHT GO CRAZY OUT HERE.

YOU KNOW, YOU THINK IT'S JUST A GHOST STORY, TILL SOMEONE TAKES IT TOO FAR.
HOW SO?
NANCY'S
FRIED CLAMS • FRENCH

I REMEMBER AN ARTICLE FROM YEARS AGO.
THEY DISCOVERED A NUDIST COLONY WAY OUT ON SQUIBNOCKET POINT. REAL REMOTE SPOT.

THE POLICE BROKE IT UP, OF COURSE.
ORDER UP!

THEN THEY STARTED FINDING ODD THINGS AROUND THE CAMP.

ETCHED ROCKS ALL ARRANGED IN PILES. QUITE PECULIAR.

THERE WAS A RUMOR THEY WERE OUT THERE WORSHIPPING THAT PHANTOM SHARK.

FOLKS GOT FREAKED OUT.
DID THE POLICE INVESTIGATE?

NAKED IS ONE THING. BUT . . .

THERE'S NO LAW THAT SAYS YOU CAN'T BE FOND OF SEA LIFE.

FORECLOSURE
OAK BLUFFS

THE WHITE CLAPBOARD HOUSES WITH THEIR OCEAN VIEWS PROMISE A PERFECT PICTURE.

BUT A CLOSER LOOK REVEALS SOMETHING MUCH DIFFERENT.

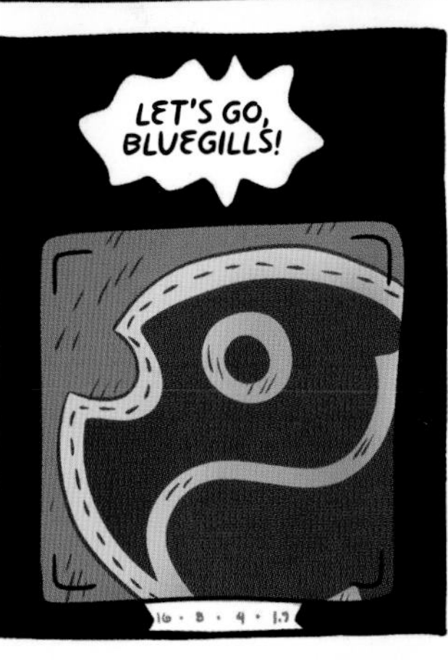
LET'S GO, BLUEGILLS!

HEY, YOU JUST RUINED MY SHOT.
OR DID I MAKE IT BETTER?

JULIA, YOU'RE SUCH A JOCK!
YOU'RE BOTH SO EMBARRASSING.
LEX

SPEAKING OF EMBARRASSING.
WHERE'D YOU DIG UP THIS OLD THING, BRIAR?!

JUST LEAVE US ALONE, LEX.
THIS PLACE HAS GOT TO BE HAUNTED.
WHEN DID YOU GET SO SERIOUS?

WHEN DID YOU GET SO LAME?

Sara

HOW'S THE ARM, BLUE STREAK?
Sara

IT'S FINE. NOT THAT YOU CARE.
WE CARE. THAT'S WHY WE'RE CHECKING TO MAKE SURE YOU'RE NOT DOING ANYTHING STUPID.

STUPID . . . LIKE DRIVING AROUND IN A CUSTOM GOLF CART?
COME ON, BRIAR, YOU LOVE THE WAVE RIPPER!

I MEAN STUPID, LIKE TRESPASSING ON PRIVATE PROPERTY.

YOU WON'T TELL ON US, WILL YOU, LEX?
GIMME A BREAK, ELIJAH. I JUST WANT TO KNOW WHAT'S GOING ON.

I'VE BEEN HEARING WEIRD THINGS.
02074
Atwood Terror
M. Grey
E. Jones
take #7

WE'RE JUST MAKING A MOVIE.
A MOVIE ABOUT A SHARK-WORSHIPPING PSYCHO?

I WONDER WHO'S DERANGED IDEA THAT WAS.

WHAT'S WRONG, ALEXANDRIA?
YOU DON'T LIKE GHOST STORIES?

WATCH IT, LEX, GHASTLY MADDIE'S GOT THAT LOOK—
HEY!

YOU DON'T GET TO CALL HER THAT.
OH NO? WHAT ARE YOU GOING TO DO?

YOU GONNA KNOCK ME DOWN?
WHOA, WHOA, WHOA.

BRIAR, WHAT'S GOING ON WITH YOU?

SHE'S TRYING TO SCARE US.

FINE, YOU WIN. WE'RE SCARED.

SCARED OF LOSING OUR PITCHER.

WE REALLY NEED YOU, BRIAR.

LET'S GO, BLUEGILLS.

SO, ARE YOU COMING WITH US OR NOT?

I ALREADY TOLD YOU, LEX.

GET LOST.

YOU GOT IT.
WAV·RIP

VROOM

LET'S DO ANOTHER TAKE.
NOT TODAY, GAYLE.

ELIJAH?

MADDIE'S RIGHT. THE WIND IS TOO STRONG. WE WON'T GET GOOD AUDIO.

RELAX, GAYLE. WE'LL TRY AGAIN TOMORROW.

"There is no sight like that of the Grand Atlantic."

ELIJAH.

MRS. DAGGETT WAS TELLING ME ABOUT YOUR MOVIE PROJECT.
HUH? BUT WE TALKED—
MOVIE FX

AND YOU NEGLECTED TO SAY IT WAS AN INVESTIGATION OF A MURDERER WHO LIVED ON THE ISLAND.

THE ATWOOD TERROR. YOU KNOW, WITH THE PHANTOM—
WE KNOW, DEAR.
MOVIE F

WE'LL BE CAREFUL.

DUKE'S HARDWARE
CLOSED

YOU KNOW, THIS MOVIE OF YOURS HAS GOT PEOPLE TALKING.
YEAH.
DUKE'S HARDWARE
CHOMP!

HOW 'BOUT A CHOMP! BAR? IT'S ON ME.
THANKS, MRS. DUKE.
I MEAN MARTHA.
CHOMP! CHOCOLATE BAR
CHOMP!

I JUST WISH PEOPLE WOULD MIND THEIR OWN BUSINESS, YOU KNOW?

HARD TO IGNORE A CAN OF WORMS ONCE IT'S BEEN OPENED.

NO ONE TOLD ME IT WAS A CAN OF WORMS!

I PROMISED MYSELF I WASN'T GONNA DO THIS, BUT NOW YOU GOT MY MEMORY TURNING.

TAKE A LOOK AT THIS GANG.
WHOA!
IS THAT YOU?

CAN YOU BELIEVE IT? I WAS PROBABLY JUST ABOUT YOUR AGE.

I WAS A REAL SCOOBY-DOO BACK THEN.
HUH?

IT WAS THE SUMMER OF THE SHARK WORSHIPPERS. ME AND MY FRIENDS GOT A BIT OBSESSED WITH THE STORY. TAKE A LOOK . . .

THIS IS A RUBBING FROM ONE OF THE ROCKS THEY FOUND ON THE BEACH. DON'T ASK HOW I GOT IT.
THE BLACK EYE!

A TRIDENT INSIDE A SHARK FIN INSIDE AN EYE.
TOOK US A WHOLE SUMMER TO FIGURE THAT OUT.

I REALLY THOUGHT WE WERE GONNA FIND THAT OL' CLUBHOUSE.

WHY'D YOU GIVE UP?

I DIDN'T GIVE UP; I GREW UP.
AND STARTED LOOKING FOR OTHER ADVENTURES.

HEY, MARTHA, COULD WE GET YOU TO TALK ABOUT THIS ON CAMERA?

SORRY, THAT'S NOT SOMETHING I WANT ON RECORD.

WHAT HAPPENED TO ALL YOUR FRIENDS?

ISLAND LIFE AIN'T FOR EVERYONE. MOST LEFT.
BUT A FEW OF US STUCK AROUND.

AND YOU'RE SURE IT'S HIM, GAYLE?
YEAH, MADDIE. I SAW THE PHOTO. IT'S SHELLY.

I DON'T THINK I'LL EVER GET USED TO ALL THE SMELLS AROUND HERE.
ELIJAH, GET THE CAMERA READY!
#2

KNOCK KNO

WELL, LOOK WHO'S BACK.

MY STORIES AIN'T FREE, REMEMBER?
ELIJAH?
YEAH, YEAH.

IT'S GONNA BE A SHORT ONE; I GOT A DELIVERY TO MAKE.

HEY, SHELLY. I NOTICED YOUR TRAPS ARE ALL WET. WHY?
SHH!
JUST FINISHED HAULING THEM IN.

THOSE ARE ALL YOURS? WOW! THERE MUST BE SIX, SEVEN —
I GOT TEN WORKIN' TRAPS RIGHT NOW.

THAT SURE IS A LOT OF LOBSTERS!
WE DON'T WANT TO WASTE YOUR TIME. WE JUST HAVE ONE QUESTION . . .
DO YOU KNOW THIS MARK?

WHERE'D YOU SEE THIS?

IT'S FROM A SHARK RITUAL, ISN'T IT?
AH, YOU'VE BEEN TALKIN' TO MARTHA.

WAIT, TELL US ABOUT THE SHARK WORSHIPPERS!

THERE WAS NO RITUAL. JUST SOME MAINLANDERS HAVIN' A BIT OF FUN.
MADE US ISLANDERS LOOK LIKE A BUNCH OF SUPERSTITIOUS FOOLS.

THAT'S ALL THERE IS TO IT.

SORRY, NO REFUNDS.

I DON'T BELIEVE YOU.

I THINK YOU KNOW MORE ABOUT THAT MARK THAN YOU'RE TELLING US.
YOU DON'T KNOW WHAT YOU'RE TALKIN' 'BOUT, GIRL.
UM, MADDIE. I'M SUPPOSED TO DO THE INTERVIEW.

TURN THAT CAMERA OFF.
DON'T DO IT, ELIJAH.

YOU'RE GOING TO TELL US THE TRUTH.

WHY'S THAT?

BECAUSE YOU HAVE TEN LOBSTER TRAPS AND I ONLY COUNTED *FIVE* PERMIT TAGS.
THE CHIEF KNOWS I ALWAYS WORK A FEW EXTRA TRAPS. I AIN'T HURTIN' NOBODY.

I BET YOUR CUSTOMERS DON'T KNOW. ESPECIALLY THE GRAND ATLANTIC.
THE DAGGETTS HAVE ALWAYS BEEN GOOD TO MY FAMILY.

THEN IMAGINE IF WORD GOT OUT THAT THE BIGGEST HOTEL ON THE ISLAND HAD BEEN BUYING ILLEGAL LOBSTERS . . .

FOR THREE GENERATIONS.

HOW GOOD WOULD THE DAGGETTS BE TO YOU AFTER THAT?

NOW ASK HIM AGAIN, GAYLE.
UH, OK.

UM, SHELLY. AH, WHAT DO YOU KNOW ABOUT THE MARK?

I KNOW IT BRINGS ME GOOD LUCK.

HE'S ONE OF THE NUDISTS!

I AIN'T A SHARK WORSHIPPER. GRANDPA PULLED IT OUT OF THE MUD WHILE HE WAS RAKING CLAMS.
AN' HE GAVE IT TO MY PA, AND PA GAVE IT TO ME.

THE STORY GOES . . .

CAPTAIN ATWOOD MARKED EACH OFFERING WITH THE BLACK EYE BEORE HE FED IT TO THE SEA.

YOU'RE SAYING THE REAL ATWOOD COULDA MARKED THAT ROCK?
ROCK? THIS IS A BIT OF FOREHEAD.

YOU MEAN, LIKE, A HUMAN FOREHEAD?
HEY, I KNOW MY BONES.

BUT HOW DO YOU—

GAYLE.

AH.

YOU FOUND ALL THOSE BONES RAKING FOR CLAMS?
THREE GENERATIONS' WORTH OF CLAMS.

SHELLY, CAN YOU SHOW US ON A MAP WHERE THE MARKED SKULLS CAME FROM?

NOW, IF I SHOW YOU, I GIVE AWAY MY FAMILY'S SECRET SHELLFISHIN' SPOT.

I'M TAKING THAT TO MY GRAVE.

YOU MUST HAVE
TOLD MARTHA DUKE
AND THOSE OTHER KIDS.

THEY WERE MY
BEST FRIENDS.

WE HAD NO
SECRETS.

IF YOU'LL EXCUSE ME,
I GOTTA GET BACK
TO WORK.

MRS. DAGGETT IS
EXPECTING ME.
ZANUCK
SINCE 1893

N
PUBLIC BEACH
SHELLY'S
SHACK
ATWOOD'S CLUBHOUSE
MUST BE SOMEWHERE
ALONG THIS BIG STRETCH
OF COASTLINE.
MENEMSHA POND
MENEMSHA

HOW DO YOU FIGURE THAT?
SHELLY'S SECRET SPOT IS DEFINITELY IN MENEMSHA POND. IT'S THE BEST SHELLFISHING ON THE ISLAND.

FUN FACT: SHARKS PUKE UP THINGS TOO BIG TO DIGEST.
LIKE A HUMAN SKULL!

ATWOOD'S SHARKS SWAM RIGHT PAST THE POND INLET.
PUKING SKULLS ALL OVER!
SHELL SHACK

HEY, MADDIE. DON'T DO THAT AGAIN.
DON'T . . . DRAW ON YOUR MAP?

I'M TALKING ABOUT WHAT YOU DID TO SHELLY. HE DIDN'T DESERVE THAT.

I'M NOT USING THE FOOTAGE.
YES, YOU ARE. THE ATWOOD MARK IS THE KEY TO THE WHOLE MOVIE.

WELL, I'M CUTTING THE LOBSTER TRAP STUFF. IT'S CRUEL.
YOU WERE KINDA MEAN, MADDIE.
GIMME A BREAK! I'M JUST FOLLOWING THE STORY. IT'S MY JOB, REMEMBER?

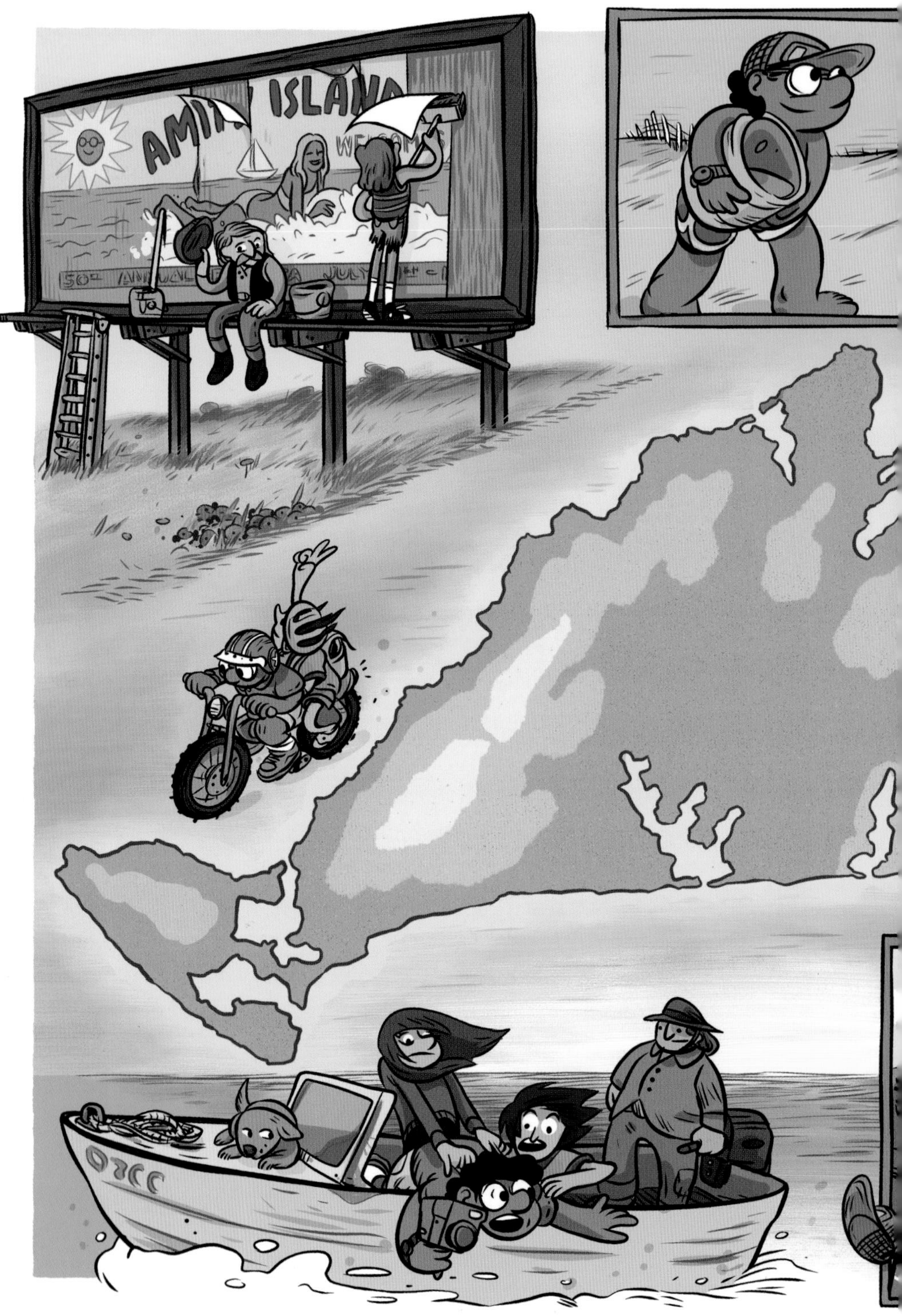

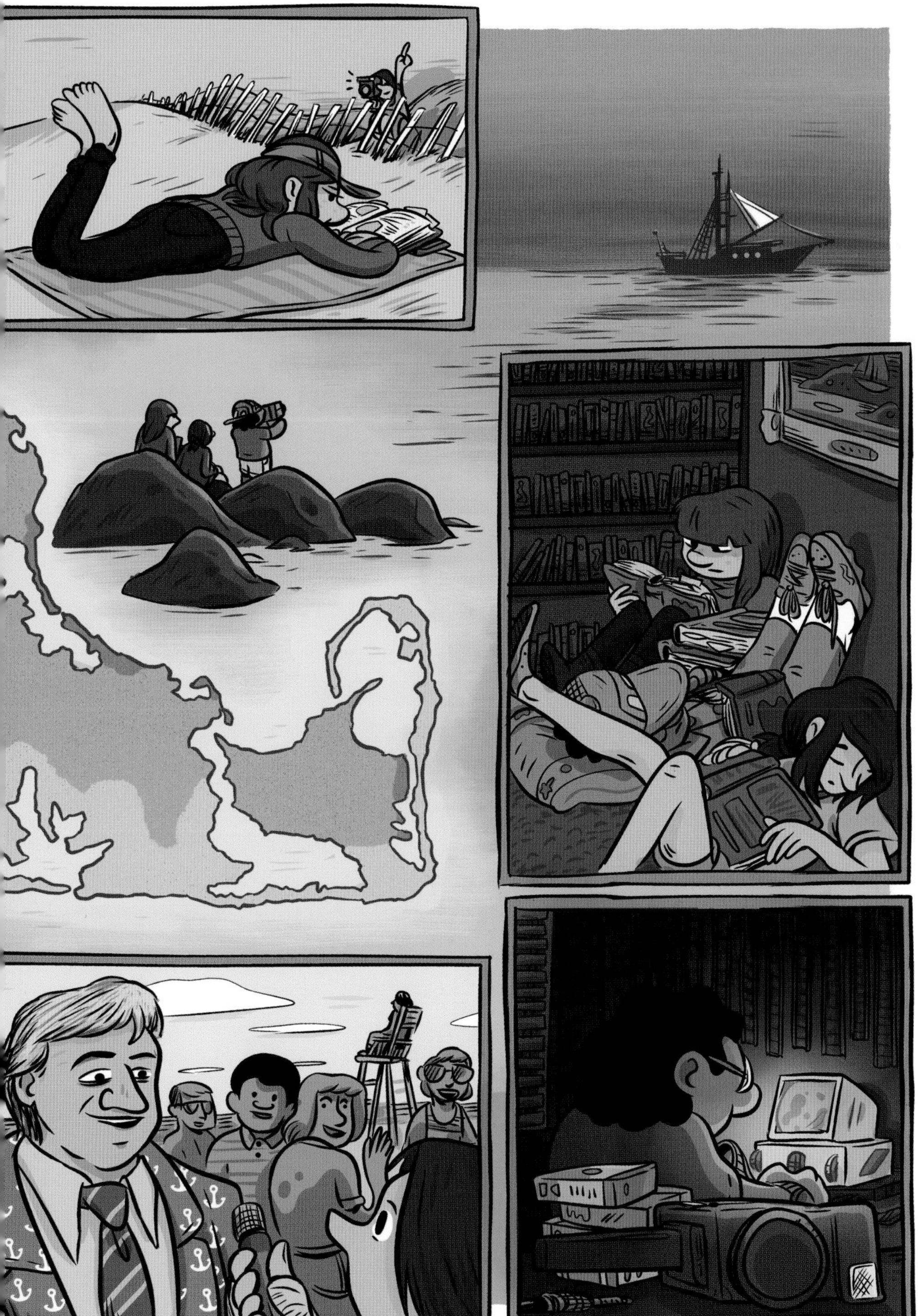

Leftovers
in the fridge.

ENJOY!

OUCH.

LAST NIGHT I FINISHED EDITING ALL OUR FOOTAGE TOGETHER!
COFFEE SHOP

SO OUR MOVIE IS DONE?!
UH, YES.

IT JUST DOESN'T HAVE AN ENDING.

ELIJAH!
HOW CAN IT BE DONE WITHOUT AN ENDING?!
I DON'T KNOW . . . I JUST HATE SAYING NO TO PEOPLE.

OF COURSE IT'S NOT FINISHED.

WE DON'T HAVE PROOF OF LEVITT ATWOOD.

HE WAS RICH. THERE'S NOT ONE PHOTO OF HIM?
ANYTHING THAT PROVES HE WAS A REAL GUY.
I'VE CHECKED EVERY HISTORY BOOK AND PUBLIC RECORD. YOU KNOW I HAVE.
THERE'S NO SIGN OF HIM.

EXCEPT HIS MARK.

WE GOTTA KEEP INTERVIEWING.
THERE'S NO ONE LEFT WHO WANTS TO TALK TO US.

SIGH.

YOU KIDS GONNA ORDER ANYTHING ELSE? THIS ISN'T A DAYCARE, YA KNOW.

OH, SORRY.
ELIJAH . . .
GOT IT.
EXPECTING A MIDMORNING RUSH, ARE YOU?

YA NEVER KNOW.

BOY, TALK ABOUT THE EVIL EYE.
WHAT'S HER PROBLEM?
WE'RE RUFFLING FEATHERS. THERE IS MORE TO THE ATWOOD STORY. WE HAVE TO KEEP LOOKING.

WE ONLY HAVE SEVEN DAYS UNTIL THE FESTIVAL. THAT'S NOT A LOT OF TIME.

MADDIE, YOU GET BACK TO YOUR RESEARCH. SEE IF THERE IS ANYTHING YOU COULDA MISSED.
OPEN
AND WHAT ARE YOU TWO GOING TO DO?

GAYLE AND I ARE OFF TO SEE THE WIZARD!

GET THOSE KIDS OFF MY SET, CHARLIE.
SHARK
GLOBAL

SORRY ABOUT THAT, STEVE.

CHARLIE!
SO WHAT DO YOU THINK?
I THINK THIS GAZEBO IS MISSING A TUBA PLAYER.

HEY, CARL. CAN YOU HELP ME OUT HERE?
I'M JUST THE PROP GUY. I DON'T DEAL IN PEOPLE.

SO WHAT DO YOU THINK ABOUT OUR PROBLEM?
IN MY EXPERIENCE, A GOOD ENDING AIN'T EASY TO COME BY.
EVER CONSIDER MAKING IT UP?

YOU MEAN LIE?

ARCADE
LIE, NO.
FICTIONALIZE, WHY NOT?
NO FICTION. MADDIE SAYS IT'S GOTTA BE REAL.

I TELL YA, YOU'VE GOT YOUR HANDS FULL WITH THAT GIRL!

GOTTA ADMIRE A DIRECTOR WITH A VISION, THOUGH.

HOLD ON THERE, CARL!

KILLER SHARK
KILLER SHARK? YOU KIDDING?
THAT'S A LITTLE ON THE NOSE, DON'T YOU THINK?

COME ON, CHARLIE! WE'RE REALLY STUCK.
OK, OK. SO THE MOVIE IS ABOUT A NUTZOID SHARK CULT MURDER, RIGHT? WHY NOT GIVE HER SOME GORE?
WE DON'T HAVE ANY GORE.
1
2
3

HEY, CAN WE BORROW YOUR SEVERED LEG?
NO CAN DO. ALL PROPS ARE PROPERTY OF GLOBAL STUDIOS. I COULD LOSE MY JOB.
GLOBAL

THESE KIDS BUGGIN' YOU, MR. POTTER? I CAN HAVE THEM REMOVED.
NAH, CHIEF. THESE "KIDS" ARE MY INTERNS.

BREAK IS OVER, FELLAS. THE SHARK SIGHTING SCENE SHOOTS IN TEN!

WHOA, IS BRUCE HERE TODAY?!
NOPE. HE AIN'T WATERPROOF QUITE YET.

HOW DO YOU FILM A SCENE ABOUT A MONSTER SHARK WITHOUT THE SHARK?

YOU DON'T HAVE TO SHOW 'EM A MONSTER TO GET 'EM SCARED.
YOU JUST GOTTA REMIND 'EM THAT IT'S OUT THERE.
WINK
EXPLOS

WE NEED YOU TO PICK OUT A RAFT, BOSS.
LET ME SEE 'EM.

CHARLIE, WE KNOW YOU CAN'T GIVE US ANY PROPS. BUT WE WERE WONDERING . . .
STEVE LIKES YELLOW.

COULD YOU SPARE A BIT OF BLOOD?

OVER A CENTURY HAS PASSED . . .
AND THE MYSTERIOUS DEATH OF CAPTAIN ATWOOD . . .
STILL HAUNTS THE ISLAND.
WE MAY NEVER KNOW WHAT HAPPENED.
BUT ONE THING IS FOR SURE . . .
ONCE YOU KNOW THE STORY OF THE ATWOOD TERROR . . .
YOU'LL NEVER GO IN THE WATER AGAIN!
THE END?

WHAT DO YOU THINK?
DID YOU LIKE ALL THE BLOOD?

TOO SCARY?

YOU TWO DON'T UNDERSTAND THIS STORY, DO YOU?

IT IS NOT ABOUT A SCARY SHARK.

THE NIGHT OF THE STORM . . .
CAPTAIN ATWOOD WENT TO THE EDGE OF THE JETTY TO FACE THE TRUTH.

TO FACE THE EVIL THINGS HE'D DONE AND WHO HE'D BECOME.

WHATEVER IT WAS THAT ROSE UP FROM THE WATER WAS MORE THAN A SHARK.

IT WAS A RECKONING.

MADDIE, YOU'RE ASKING ME TO FILM SOMETHING THAT WE CAN'T EVEN SEE.

I KNOW.
BUT MAYBE I HAVE THE NEXT BEST THING.

WHOA! THIS MAP IS ANCIENT.
MY DAD'S OBSESSED WITH OLD MAPS OF THE ISLAND. I "BORROWED" THIS ONE.

ISN'T IT . . . LIKE, VALUABLE?
IT'S FOR A GOOD CAUSE, RIGHT?

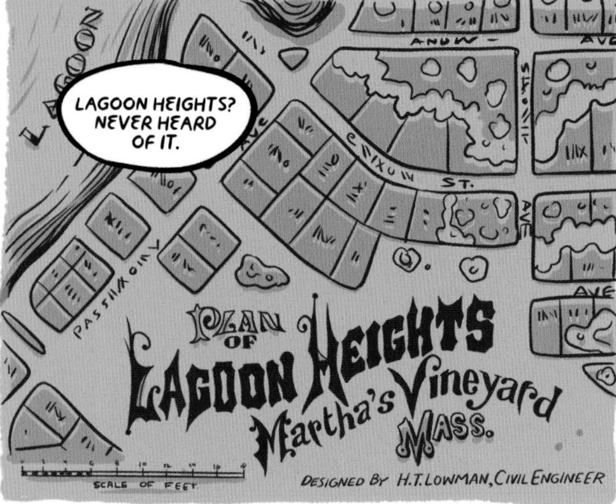
LAGOON HEIGHTS? NEVER HEARD OF IT.
PLAN OF LAGOON HEIGHTS
Martha's Vineyard Mass.
SCALE OF FEET
DESIGNED BY H.T. LOWMAN, CIVIL ENGINEER

IT'S A PLAN FOR A HOUSING DEVELOPMENT FROM 1880.
1880 . . . THAT'S AROUND WHEN ATWOOD DIED. PROBABLY.

EXACTLY. CHECK OUT THIS CEMETERY HERE.
LOT 32
LOT 31
LOT 33
LOT 28
LOT 29
LOT 30
DAVIS
ST.
VINEYARD NATIONAL CEMETERY
LOT 52
LOT 51
CHARD
LOT 54
LOT 55

AFTER 1880, IT COMPLETELY DISAPPEARS FROM ALL MAPS AND RECORDS. NO ONE KNOWS WHO'S BURIED IN IT.
LAGOON
PLAN OF LAGOON HEIGHTS Martha's Vineyard MASS.
H.T. LOWMAN CIVIL ENGINE

THIS SYMBOL MEANS IT'S A MILITARY CEMETERY.
ATWOOD'S GRAVE IS THERE. I KNOW IT.
WHOA. ACTUAL PROOF.

THIS IS THE ENDING WE NEED.

ATWOOD TERROR MOVIE
1 2 3 4 5 6
I DUNNO. I LIKE THE SHARK FIN ENDING.

COME ON, ELIJAH! WE HAVE TO AT LEAST CHECK IT OUT.
I KNOW. FOLLOW THE STORY. RIGHT.

VROOM!

WHAT'S UP, CAMERAMAN?
OH, HELLO.
WAV-RIP

HEY, ELIJAH. WE SET UP A PROJECTOR IN THE CONFERENCE ROOM. WANNA WATCH A MOVIE?
NO THANKS.

COME ON, WE GOT EIGHT DIFFERENT KINDS OF CHIPS!
YEAH, I'M JUST NOT IN THE MOOD FOR A MOVIE.

DID YOU CATCH YOUR PHANTOM SHARK YET?
NO, NOT YET.

WE'RE STILL LOOKING. MADDIE'S A BIT OBSESSED.
YEAH. WATCH OUT FOR HER. SHE'S A BIT NUTS.

HEY, I SHOULDN'T BE TELLING YOU THIS . . .

I HEARD THE DIRECTOR AND CREW TALKING AT BREAKFAST.

APPARENTLY, THEIR BIG SHARK ROBOT IS READY.

BRUCE IS FINALLY WATERPROOF!

AND SOMETHING ABOUT THE WHARF. "TOMORROW, AFTER MIDNIGHT."
MAKES SENSE, THEY WANT TO AVOID THE PRESS.

HOLD ON.
WHY ARE YOU TELLING ME THIS?

'CAUSE YOU NEED A SHARK. AND 'CAUSE YOU'RE GAYLE'S FRIEND.
IF YOU CAN HELP HER FINISH HER MOVIE . . .

MAYBE SHE CAN STOP HATING ME.

HEY, WHAT MOVIE ARE YOU WATCHING?

AMERICAN SPRAYPAINT.

HEY, LEX!
WAIT UP!
WAV-RIP

WELCOME TO LAGOON HEIGHTS.
THE VINEYARD'S MOST UP-AND-COMING NEIGHBORHOOD.
NO WONDER YOU NEVER HEARD OF IT. IT NEVER EXISTED!
WELL, I THINK IT'S A PERFECT PLACE TO LIVE.

IF YOU'RE A LEECH, SNAKE, SNAPPING TURTLE, ALLIGATOR . . .

I TOLD YOU: "WEAR BOOTS."
I DON'T OWN SWAMP BOOTS!
SHE DID SAY THAT.

WE'VE BEEN OUT HERE FOR HOURS, MADDIE. WHERE'S THE CEMETERY?
I THINK WE'RE STANDING IN IT.

WE'RE LOOKING FOR A NAVAL OFFICER'S TOMB.
KEEP AN EYE OUT FOR NAUTICAL ENGRAVINGS.

HEY . . . THIS BIRD IS STARING AT ME!

STOP GOOFING AROUND, GAYLE. WE'RE BURNING DAYLIGHT.

WHO SAYS "BURNING DAYLIGHT"?
MOVIE CREWS!

HEY!
I FOUND SOMETHING!

HOLD ON, I'M GETTING THE CAMERA.
I CAN SEE AN ANCHOR.
THAT'S AN ANCHOR?

GAYLE, START DIGGING.
WHAT?
IN MEMORY OF

THIS IS WHERE THE OBSESSIVE INTERVIEWER UNCOVERS THE TRUTH OF CAPTAIN ATWOOD.
WE NEED TO FILM THE BIG REVEAL.

SO NOW I'M OBSESSIVE, HUH?

JUST DIG.

MEMO

CAN YOU DIG FASTER? IT'S GETTING DARK.
IN CASE YOU FORGOT, I ONLY HAVE ONE ARM.

SORRY, GUYS. I HIT A ROOT. FEELS LIKE A BIG ONE.
IN MEMORY OF CAPTAIN

YOU GOTTA BE KIDDING ME.
TAKE IT EASY, MADDIE.

WHAT IS IT?!
MY LENS! YOU GOT MUD ON IT!

JUST WIPE IT OFF.
ARE YOU CRAZY?! THIS IS A LIMITED-EDITION DAS ZOOM-OBJEKTIV LENS! I COULD SCRATCH IT!

YOU MUST HAVE BROUGHT A BACKUP.
NO, I DID NOT BRING A BACKUP!

ELIJAH, WE NEED THIS ENDING.

WRONG, MADDIE.
YOU NEED THIS ENDING.

I LIKE THE ENDING WE ALREADY HAVE.
YOU CAN'T BE SERIOUS. THEY'D LAUGH US OUT OF THE MOVIE THEATER.

NOT IF WE HAD BRUCE IN OUR MOVIE.
THE ROBOT SHARK? NOW YOU'RE DREAMING.

I AM NOT! IN FACT, I GOT A TIP THAT BRUCE IS READY FOR FILMING AND HE'LL BE AT THE WHARF AT MIDNIGHT.

OH REALLY? WHO GAVE YOU THAT CONVENIENT TIP?
I CAN'T REVEAL MY SOURCE.

ELIJAH.
ARE YOU REALLY THAT GULLIBLE?

GEESH, MADDIE. YOU ACT LIKE SOMEONE'S OUT TO GET US.

UM...

YOU KNOW, WE'RE RUNNING OUT OF TIME.
EXCLUSIVE FOOTAGE OF BRUCE IS OUR BEST SHOT AT WINNING THE FILM FESTIVAL.

SNEAKING AROUND IS ONLY GOING TO GET US ONE THING:
TROUBLE.

THE SHARK ISN'T THE STORY. ATWOOD IS THE STORY.
WE'RE COMING BACK AT DAWN WITH A SHOVEL AND WE'LL FINISH DIGGING.

IT'S MY CAMERA!
AND I'M YOUR DIRECTOR!

WHY ARE YOU FIGHTING?! WE ALL WANT THE SAME THING, RIGHT?

YEAH.
I SUPPOSE.

WE DON'T HAVE TO CHOOSE AN ENDING.

NOT YET.

TONIGHT WE GO SEE BRUCE.
TOMORROW WE COME BACK WITH A SHOVEL.
IN MEMORY OF

THEN WE DECIDE TOGETHER.

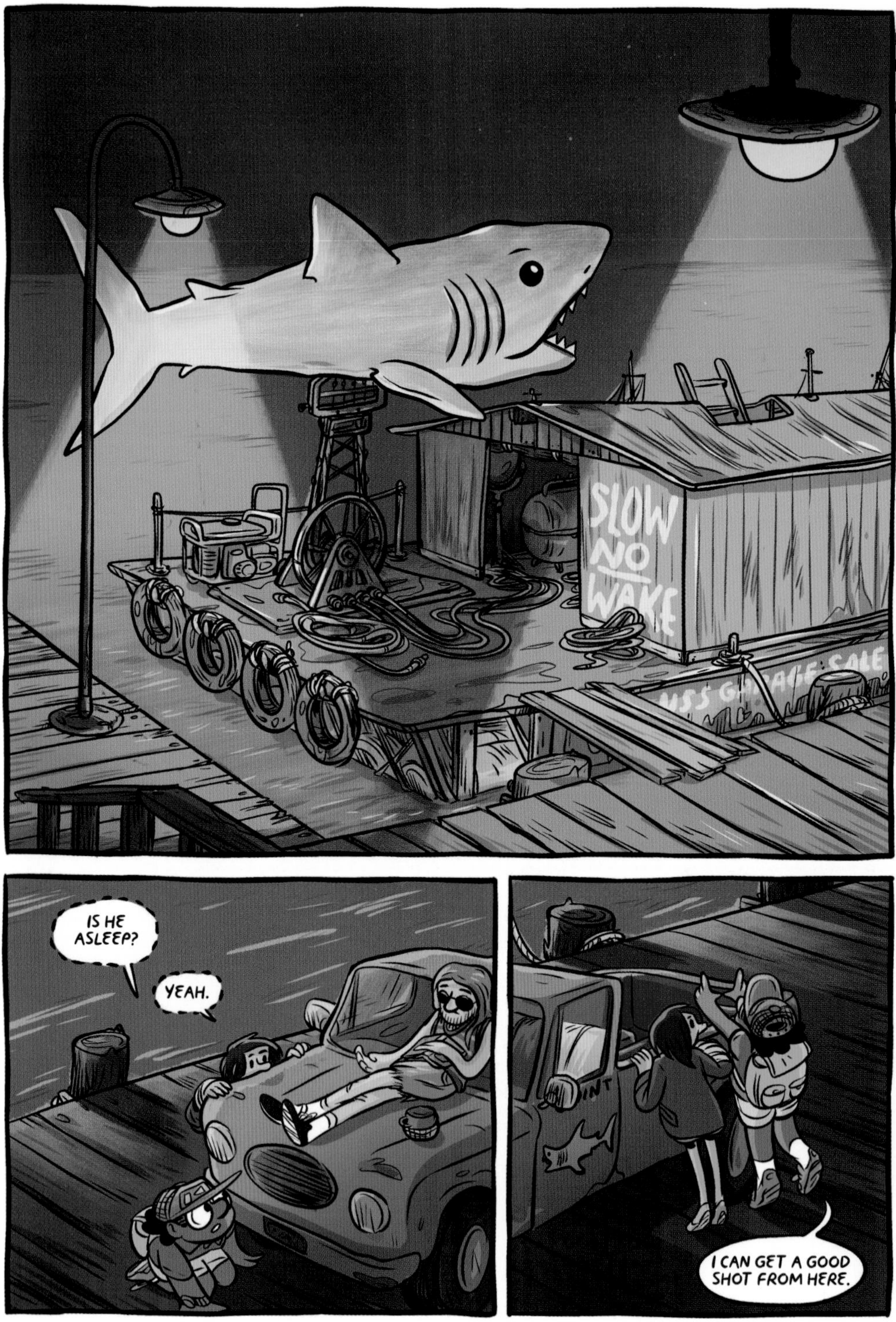

SLOW
NO
WAKE

IS HE ASLEEP?
YEAH.

I CAN GET A GOOD SHOT FROM HERE.

THIS DOESN'T FEEL RIGHT WITHOUT MADDIE HERE.
SHE'S THE ONE WHO DECIDED NOT TO SHOW UP.

I KNOW.
BUT WE STILL NEED TO FOLLOW HER STORY.

OK, SO HOW DO WE DO THAT?
MADDIE SAYS ATWOOD CALLED HIMSELF . . .

FOLLOWER OF THE BLACK EYE.

THE WAR TURNED HIS SOUL BLACK AND LIFELESS.

JUST LIKE THE EYE OF A SHARK.

IF SHE WERE HERE, MADDIE WOULD TELL YOU TO GET A CLOSE-UP.

I SEE A LADDER. YOU CAN CLIMB UP TO BRUCE THERE.

YOU'RE SHAKING, WHAT'S WRONG?
I'M SCARED OF HEIGHTS.

IT'S, LIKE, EIGHT FEET, ELIJAH!
THEN I'M SCARED OF LADDERS! YOU KNOW I HAVE AWFUL BALANCE.

IT'S OK. I CAN DO IT.

YOU THINK WE REALLY NEED THIS SHOT?
YEAH, I DO.

WATCH PROP GUY.
IF HE MOVES, SHINE THE FLASHLIGHT.
QUINT

BE CAREFUL, GAYLE.
I WON'T BREAK YOUR PRECIOUS CAMERA.

THAT'S NOT WHAT I MEANT.

SLOW NO WAKE

SLOW NO WAKE

OH, HELLO.

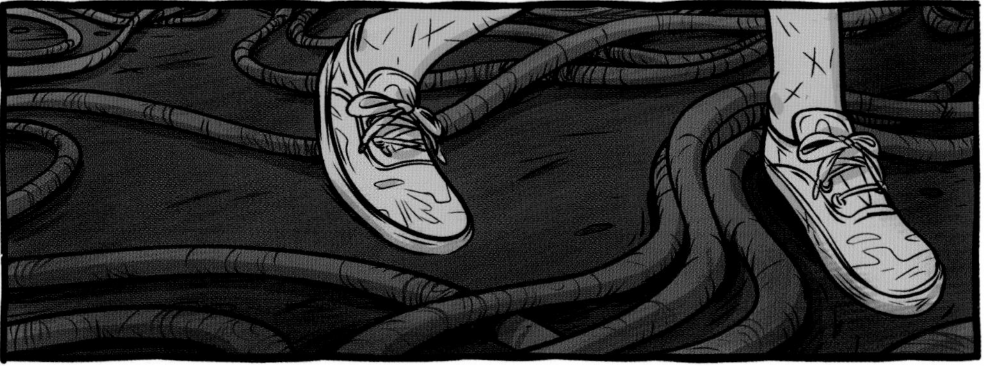

THIS IS THE POLICE!
YOU ARE TRESPASSING ON PRIVATE PROPERTY!
COME OUT WITH YOUR HANDS UP!

OOF!

I REPEAT, COME OUT WITH YOUR HANDS UP!
I'M TRYING!
AIR
DIVE

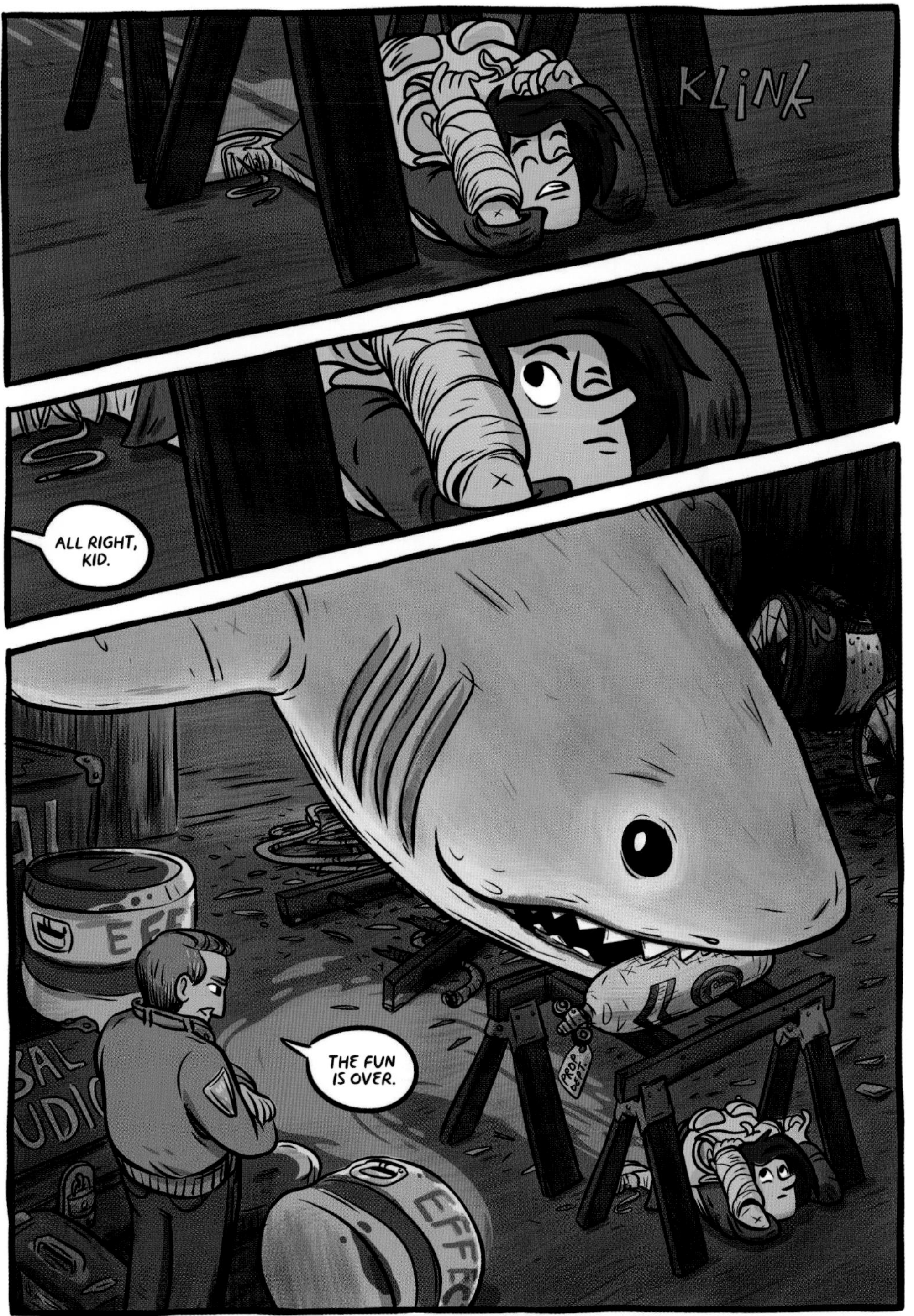
KLINK
ALL RIGHT, KID.
THE FUN IS OVER.
PROP DEPT.

WHERE'S YOUR FRIEND?
THE TALL ONE.
IT'S JUST US.
ARE WE GOING TO JAIL, SIR?

KIDS DON'T GO TO JAIL.
THEY GO HOME WITH THEIR PARENTS.

HEY, BOSS, I FOUND THIS LYING ON THE DOCK.
DID YOU TWO FILM MY SHARK?

WE'RE SORRY, CHARLIE.

YOU KNOW THE RULES, DUDES.
SIGH.

WOULD YOU LIKE TO FILE A REPORT, MR. POTTER?
THAT WON'T BE NECESSARY.

I'D LIKE TO JUST FORGET THIS EVER HAPPENED.

I DON'T GET IT . . . HOW DID THE CHIEF GET HERE SO FAST?

DID YOU TELL ANYONE WE WERE GONNA BE HERE?
NO WAY.

ELIJAH?
WHO TOLD YOU THE SHARK WAS AT THE WHARF?

SHE SAID SHE WANTED TO HELP.

LEX.
SHE SET US UP.

I KNOW. I SHOULD HAVE TOLD YOU.

I RUINED THE MOVIE, DIDN'T I?

CAN YOU JUST SAY SOMETHING?

ELIJAH JONES.

SEE YOU LATER, TRAITOR.

GAYLE!

I'M SORRY I TOOK SO LONG; I WAS AT THE HOTEL.

IT'S OK, KIDDO. I'M NOT MAD.
I'M JUST GLAD YOU'RE SAFE.

MOM.
MY ARM REALLY HURTS.

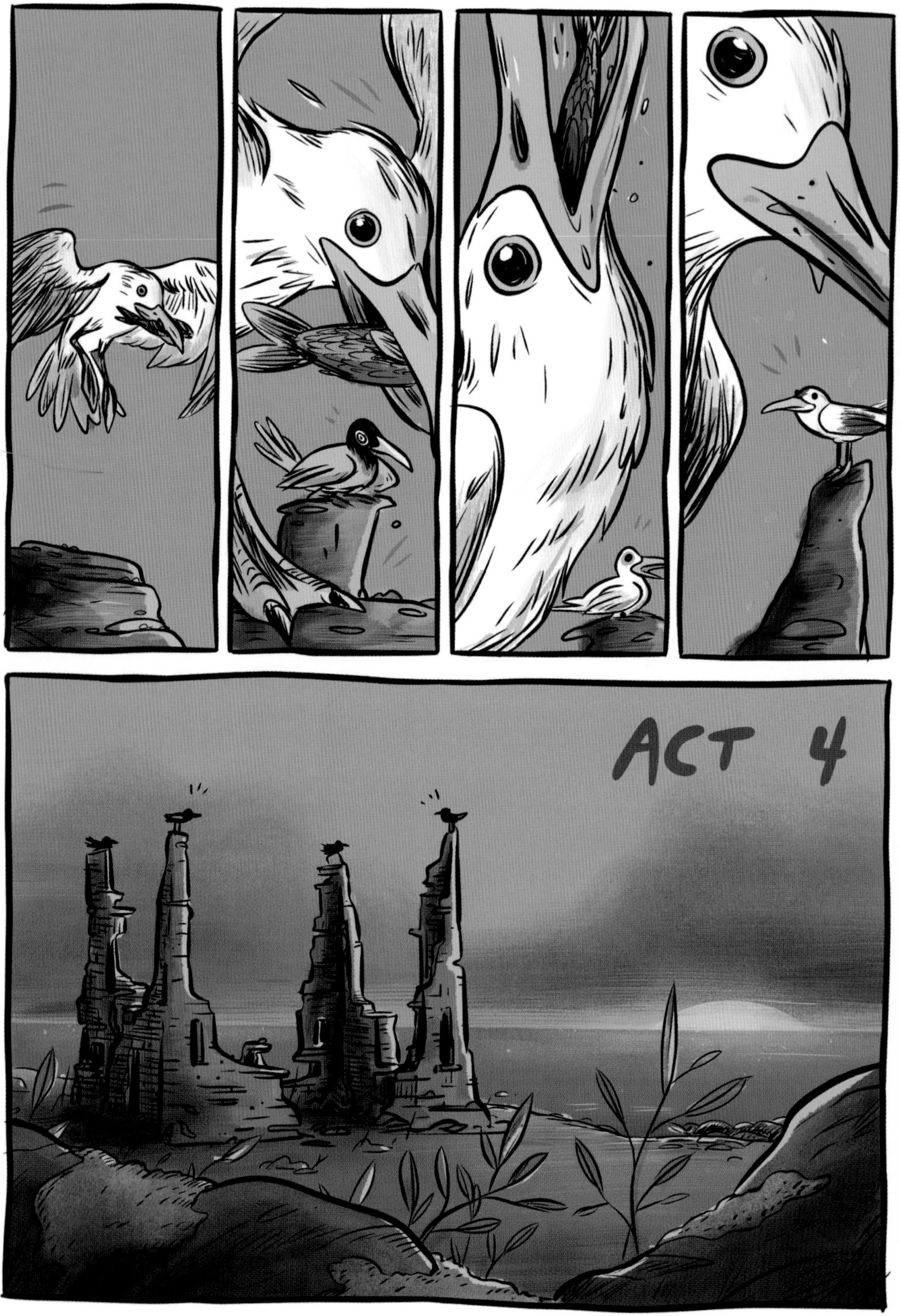

ACT 4

SAVE ME.

GRANDMA USED TO SAY:
"NEVER MEASURE, JUST WATCH THE COLOR."

YOU'RE WATCHING FOR A VERY PARTICULAR SHADE OF PURPLE.

IF YOU'RE NOT CAREFUL, THE FLAVOR OF THE ELDERBERRIES BECOMES OVERWHELMING.

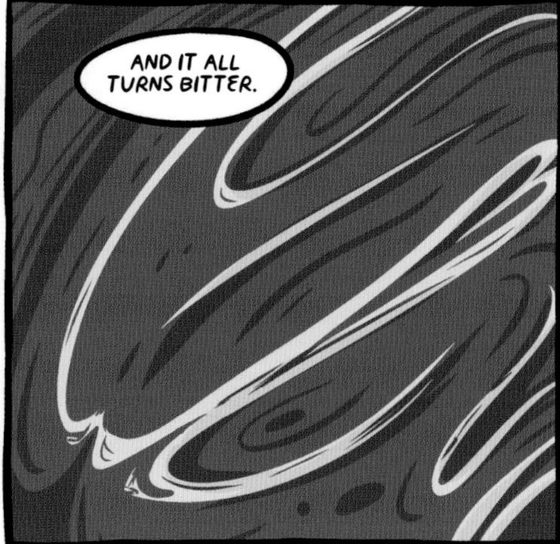
AND IT ALL TURNS BITTER.

I USED TO LOVE WATCHING GRANDMA MAKE ICE CREAM.

DO YOU REMEMBER HER? YOU WERE SO YOUNG.
I REMEMBER PICKING BERRIES . . .

I REMEMBER GRANDMA CALLING MY NAME IF I WENT TOO FAR INTO THE BUSHES.

YOU WERE A GOOD KID. YOU ALWAYS CAME RUNNING.
I NEVER DID.

I REMEMBER YOU FIGHTING WITH HER.
WE WEREN'T FIGHTING; SHE JUST WORRIED ABOUT ME SO MUCH.

YOU WORRY ABOUT ME, TOO, DON'T YOU?

YEAH.

THAT'S NOT YOUR JOB. YOU KNOW, IT'S OK TO JUST BE A KID.
I KNOW.
I JUST LIKE TO SEE YOU HAPPY.

I LIKE TO SEE YOU HAPPY, TOO.

BUT I CAN SEE YOU NEED TO GET THERE ON YOUR OWN.

MOM? DON'T CRY!

I'M SO PROUD OF YOU. EVERY DAY. ALL THE TIME.
I'M JUST REALLY MISSING YOU THIS SUMMER.

KNOCK! KNOCK!

HEY.
HI.

PUTT
PUTT
PUTT
HAVE FUN, GIRLS!
HELLO, MS. BRIAR!

I CAN'T BELIEVE YOUR MOM IS LETTING YOU SLEEP OVER AFTER THE WHOLE SHARK DEBACLE.
I KNOW.
I THINK SHE FEELS BAD FOR ME.

NEW CAST? WHAT HAPPENED?
THE DOCTOR SAID I HAD A THING CALLED A NONUNION.

WHICH MEANS THE BONES WEREN'T HEALING RIGHT, SO HE HAD TO RESET THE BREAK.
OH, GAYLE!

WHAT ABOUT PITCHING?
I DON'T KNOW.

HE JUST SAID,
"WE'LL SEE."

UGH.

I'M SORRY I DIDN'T COME THAT NIGHT. I SHOULDN'T HAVE ABANDONED MY CREW.
I'M GLAD YOU DIDN'T. IT WAS A STUPID IDEA.
WE SHOULD HAVE STUCK WITH YOUR STORY.

WEST CHOP LIGHTHOUSE
est. 1891

BEDROOM

KITCHEN

STOREROOM

45 ft.

HIGH WATER

DOWNSTAIRS IS MOSTLY OVERFLOW FROM MY DAD'S LIBRARY.
BUT I GET THE TOP FLOORS ALL TO MYSELF.
8th GRADE SPRING

GOTHIC REVIVAL ARCHITECTURE OF NEW ENGLAND.
THAT ONE HAS COOL SCHEMATIC DRAWINGS.
8th GRADE

YOU READ THIS? FOR FUN?
HEH. NOT EXACTLY. MY DAD LETS ME PICK MY TEXTBOOKS.

SO YOU BASICALLY LIVE AT SCHOOL.
GOTHIC REVIVAL ARCHITECTURE OF NEW ENGLAND

I NEVER THOUGHT OF IT THAT WAY.

BUT YEAH. I VERY MUCH DO.

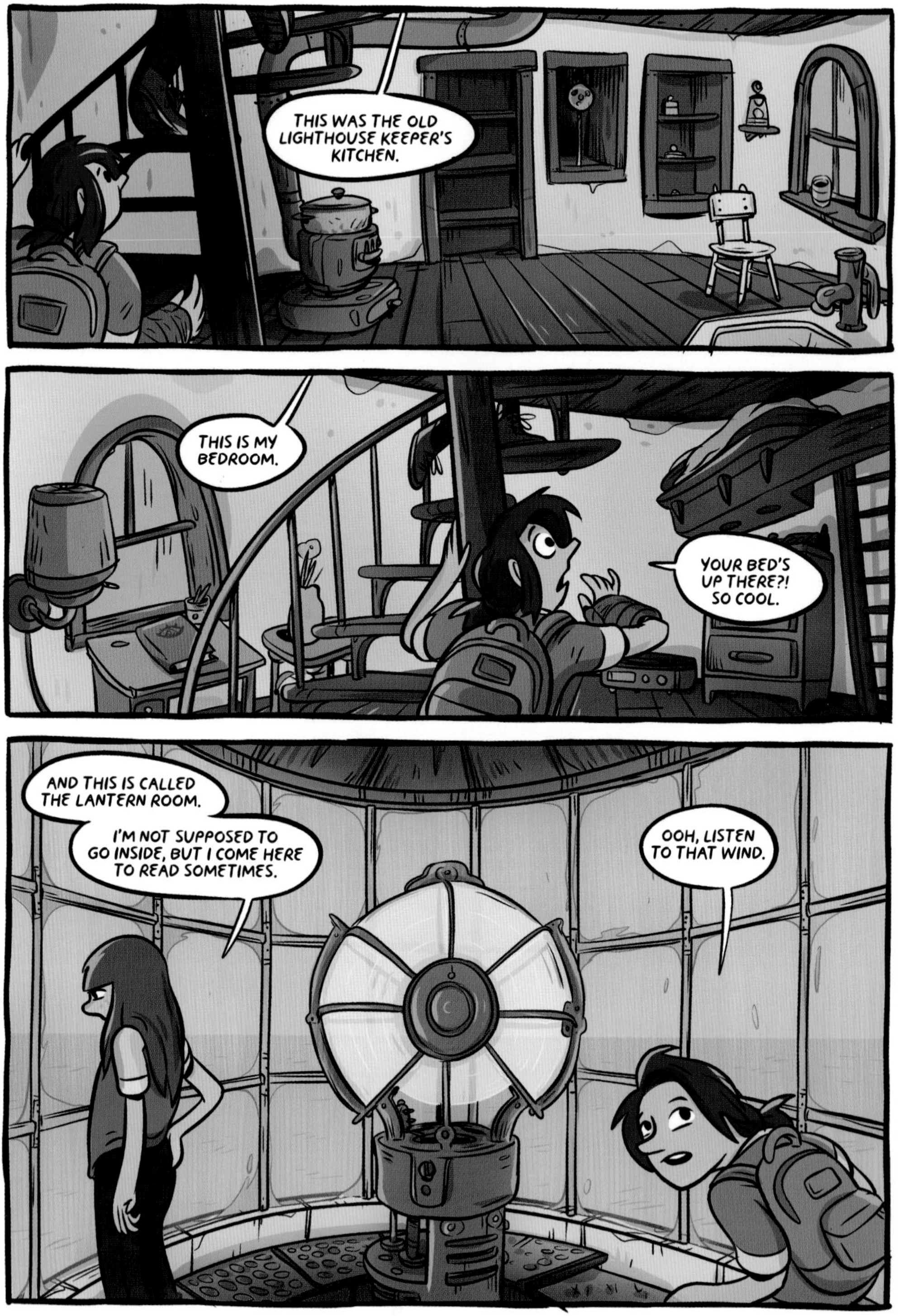

AND THIS IS CALLED THE LANTERN ROOM.
I'M NOT SUPPOSED TO GO INSIDE, BUT I COME HERE TO READ SOMETIMES.
OOH, LISTEN TO THAT WIND.

I CAN SEE VINEYARD PREP FROM HERE.

I CAN'T BELIEVE SCHOOL STARTS IN TWO WEEKS.
I'D DIE BEFORE I SET FOOT IN THERE AGAIN.

YOU WENT TO VINEYARD?
UNTIL FOURTH GRADE.

WHY'D YOU LEAVE?

ONE DAY I WOKE UP WITH THESE TWO BEAUTIES.

MAYBE I ALWAYS HAD THEM, I DON'T KNOW.
I JUST REMEMBER SHOWING UP AT SCHOOL THAT MORNING . . .

ALEXANDRIA DAGGETT POINTING AT MY NECK, AND SHOUTING . . .

"VAMPIRE!"

THEN SHE CALLED ME GHASTLY MADDIE.
AND FOR WHATEVER REASON, IT STUCK.

BY THE END OF THAT DAY SOMEONE HAD WRITTEN IT ON MY LOCKER.
GHASTLY MADDIE

DID YOU TELL YOUR PARENTS?
YEAH.
THEY TOLD ME "IT'LL BLOW OVER."

GROWN-UPS ALWAYS SAY THAT.
I TRIED, YOU KNOW? TO IGNORE THE TEASING.

THAT MADE LEX FURIOUS.

THE TEASING STOPPED, BUT I COULD FEEL ALL OF MY CLASSMATES QUIETLY HATING ME.

IT WAS LIKE I'D BEEN EXILED. FOR WEEKS, I'D COME HOME FROM SCHOOL AND CRY IN MY ROOM.

I CRIED SO MUCH I EVEN STARTED TO HATE MYSELF.

ONE DAY, I WAS SITTING IN THE PARK AND AN EGG HIT ME ON THE HEAD.
I TURNED AROUND AND THERE WAS LEX AND HER CREW. SHE WAS STARING AT ME WITH SUCH ANGER.

THEN I REALIZED, I WASN'T LIVING UP TO THE MONSTER SHE WANTED ME TO BE.

SO I GAVE HER WHAT SHE WANTED.
WHAT DID YOU DO?

I WALKED OVER AND BIT HER NECK.
YOU BIT LEX?! OH MY GOSH, YOU ARE A VAMPIRE!

DID YOU MAKE HER BLEED?
NO.
IT WAS JUST A NIBBLE.

GIRLS!
TIME FOR DINNER!
COMING!

SO THEN WHAT?
HER PARENTS FREAKED OUT. OBVIOUSLY.

AND VINEYARD PREP REVOKED MY SCHOLARSHIP THE NEXT DAY.

YOU MUST HATE HER FOR THAT.
HM.

HEY, WE SHOULD HEAD DOWN.
BUT THANKS FOR LISTENING TO ME.

I KNEW YOU'D UNDERSTAND.

WHOOOOMMMM

I'M TELLING YOU, IT WAS GIGANTIC!
DON'T BELIEVE HER, GAYLE!

I DIDN'T KNOW YOU COULD FIT SO MANY VEGETABLES IN ONE BOWL.
THAT'S DONALD. EVEN HIS COOKING IS EDUCATIONAL.

SO GAYLE, I HEAR YOU'RE FROM BOSTON ORIGINALLY?
DORCHESTER, ACTUALLY.

OH! I WAS A CIVIL ENGINEER THERE FOR FIVE YEARS!
THERE ARE SOME SIGNIFICANT BUILDINGS IN THAT NEIGHBORHOOD, YOU KNOW. I'M SURE YOU'VE VISITED THE JAMES BLAKE HOUSE.

A SIMPLE TWO-STORY WITH CLAPBOARD SIDING AND DIAMOND-PANED CASEMENT WINDOWS.
BUILT IN 1661, I BELIEVE.

JAMES WHO?
NO ONE GETS EXCITED ABOUT POSTMEDIEVAL ARCHITECTURE LIKE RHONDA DOES.

HEY, DID YOU KNOW GAYLE AND HER MOTHER ARE OPENING AN ICE-CREAM SHOP DOWN ON THE WHARF?
MADDIE . . .

WELL, THAT'S EXCITING.
I'M A BIG SUPPORTER OF LOCAL FLAVOR.

ESPECIALLY CHOCOLATE.
OH DONALD.
SO VERY FUNNY.

MOM ACTUALLY WON AN AWARD FOR HER FLAVOR ELDERBERRY OUTBURST.

HE WANTS YOU TO FOLLOW HIM.

WHERE ARE WE GOING?
WE CALL IT "THE MAP ROOM."

WHAT'S IN THE MAP ROOM?
YOU'RE BEING RHETORICAL, RIGHT?
VINEYARD HISTORICAL

OH MY GOSH, I CAN'T BELIEVE HE REMEMBERS.

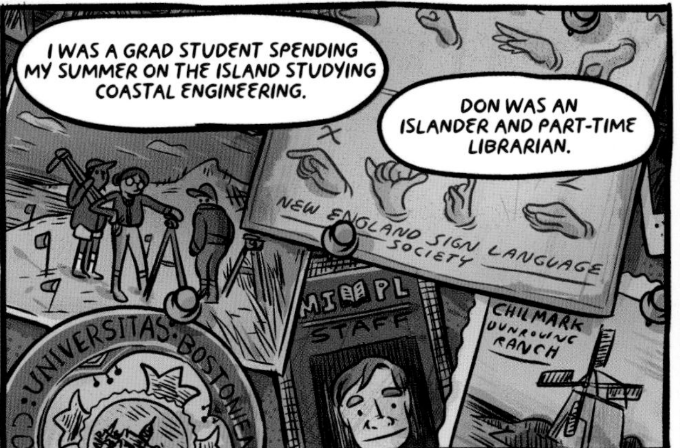
I WAS A GRAD STUDENT SPENDING MY SUMMER ON THE ISLAND STUDYING COASTAL ENGINEERING.
DON WAS AN ISLANDER AND PART-TIME LIBRARIAN.
NEW ENGLAND SIGN LANGUAGE SOCIETY
STAFF
CHILMARK
RANCH
UNIVERSITAS BOSTONIE

HE KNEW THE ISLAND, SO I ASKED HIM TO SHOW ME AROUND.

HE THOUGHT HE'D TRY AND CHARM ME BY TAKING ME TO THIS SECRET BEACH.
NAUTICAL CHARTS
TIDE CHARTS
1900-1950 TOPOGRAPHIC CHARTS

YOU COULD ONLY GET THERE DURING LOW TIDE. WHICH MEANS THE DEER DON'T BOTHER IT.

THE DUNES WERE COVERED IN ELDERBERRY BUSHES. IT WAS SO LOVELY.

REMEMBER?
I REMEMBER.

HEY, I DIDN'T KNOW THAT STORY.
NOW YOU DO.

LOCAL ELDERBERRIES! MY MOM WILL LOVE THAT.

THE BEACH IS JUST EAST OF MENEMSHA POND.
Menemsha Pond

THERE'S NO ROAD, JUST AN OLD HIKING TRAIL. THERE WAS A SIGN . . .
WHAT DID IT SAY, DON?

"STONE PILLARS." YES, THAT'S RIGHT.

WHAT?
DON SAYS, "BE CAREFUL."

HE'S RIGHT — WHEN THE EASTERN WINDS SHIFT, THAT STRETCH OF COASTLINE GETS SOME MONSTROUS WAVES.
THANK YOU, PARENTAL ADVISORY BOARD.

WE ADVISE BECAUSE WE CARE.
GROAN. DO YOU TWO MIND IF MY FRIEND AND I HAVE A NORMAL SLEEPOVER?

MRS. GREY, YOU SAID "STONE PILLARS."
PILLARS FOR WHAT?

THAT'S A GOOD QUESTION!
IF I RECALL, THE NAME IS REFERRING TO THE RUINS OF AN OLD STONE FOUNDATION.

ONLY A FEW OF THE EARLY ISLANDERS COULD AFFORD TO RAISE HURRICANE-PROOF HOMES AND BUILDINGS.

IT'S MOST LIKELY SOME RICH MAN'S FISHING CLUB.

OK, DON. LET'S DO THE DISHES AND LEAVE THESE GIRLS ALONE.

351
350
351
B.

351
350
351
B.

OH MY GOD. THE SUN IS COMING UP.
ISLANDIA

WE STAYED UP ALL NIGHT . . . STARING AT MAPS?!

YOU KNOW, MADDIE, THIS IS NOT HOW SLEEPOVERS ARE SUPPOSED TO GO.
FINE. GO TO BED.

IT'S TOO LATE FOR THAT, NOW ISN'T IT?
YOU MEAN TOO EARLY.

I MEAN TOO LATE. LET'S DO THE MATH.
THE STONE PILLAR TRAIL IS A FOUR-MILE STRETCH OF OVERGROWN BEACH.

THERE ARE EIGHT HISTORIC FISHING CLUBS MARKED ALONG THE TRAIL.
8 CLUBS
4 MILES

THE FESTIVAL DEADLINE IS IN T MINUS 13 HOURS AND COUNTING.
8 CLUBS
13 HOURS
4 MILES

YOU HAVE TWO BICYCLES, I HAVE ONE ARM, WE BOTH HAVE HAD ZERO SLEEP.
Ø SLEEP
13 HOURS

WHAT'S UP WITH YOU? I THOUGHT YOU NEEDED THAT PRIZE MONEY.

I DO.
BUT IT JUST SEEMS IMPOSSIBLE.
IT HAS ALWAYS SEEMED IMPOSSIBLE.

YET HERE WE ARE.
CLOSER THAN EVER.

HARBOR INN SIGN - 1840

HISTORICAL STAINED GLASS - 1844

DECORATIVE HOOKED RUG - 1877

EARLY COLORIZED PHOTOGRAPH - 1898

VIEW FROM MENEMSHA INN ROAD.

THE PHOTO HAS A LABEL.

MENEMSHA INN ROAD. WHERE IS THAT?
I'M LOOKING.

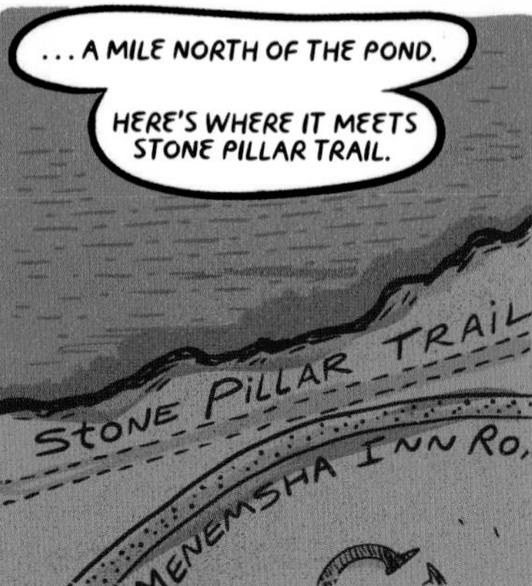
. . . A MILE NORTH OF THE POND.
HERE'S WHERE IT MEETS STONE PILLAR TRAIL.
STONE PILLAR TRAIL
MENEMSHA INN RO.

WE FIND THAT SPOT. WE FIND THE CLUBHOUSE.
BUT WE NEED ELIJAH TO FINISH THE MOVIE.

I HAVE TO TELL YOU . . .
I CALLED HIM A TRAITOR.

WE'LL DEAL WITH THAT WHEN WE GET TO THE HOTEL.

OH MAN.
WHAT'S WRONG?

MY DAD IS GONNA KILL ME FOR THIS.

DRRRIIIPPP

SO THAT'S WHAT THEY MEAN BY . . .
BALANCED BREAKFAST.

OH, HEY.
HI.

WE FOUND
THE CLUBHOUSE.

OH.

MY DAD ASKED ME TO GO TO ISLAND FEST WITH HIM THIS AFTERNOON.
I'M GOING TO FILM HIS INTERVIEWS.

THAT'S GREAT, ELIJAH. IT'S WHAT YOU WANTED ALL ALONG.
SORRY I CAN'T GO WITH YOU.

I WOULDN'T WANT TO BETRAY HIM, TOO.

IT'S OK. WE COMPLETELY UNDERSTAND.

ENJOY YOUR BREAKFAST AND WE'LL SEE YOU LATER.

SEE, I TOLD YOU:
IMPOSSIBLE!

YET HERE WE ARE.

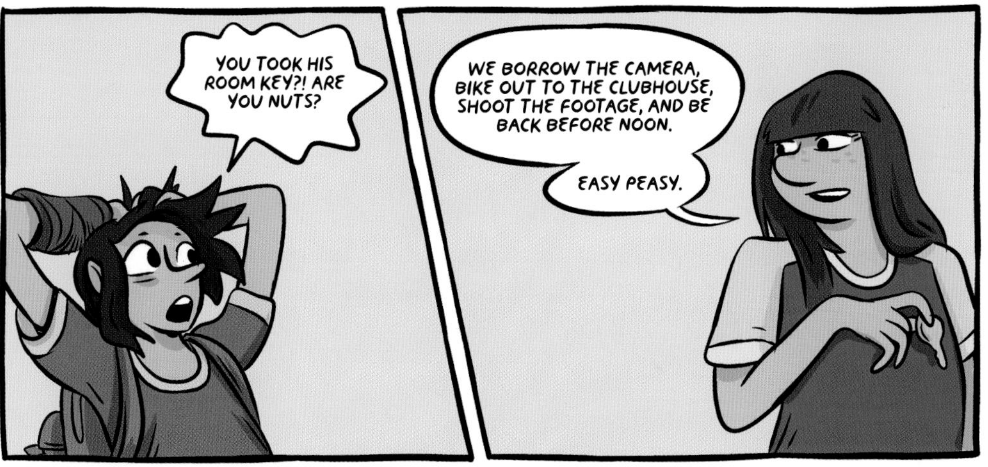
YOU TOOK HIS ROOM KEY?! ARE YOU NUTS?
WE BORROW THE CAMERA, BIKE OUT TO THE CLUBHOUSE, SHOOT THE FOOTAGE, AND BE BACK BEFORE NOON.
EASY PEASY.

EASY, EXCEPT THAT WHEN HE FINDS OUT WE "BORROWED" HIS CAMERA, HE'S GOING TO KILL US.

SO WHAT, WE GIVE UP? COME ON, GAYLE, ELIJAH NEEDS THIS MOVIE AS MUCH AS YOU DO.

LET'S PROVE IT TO HIM.

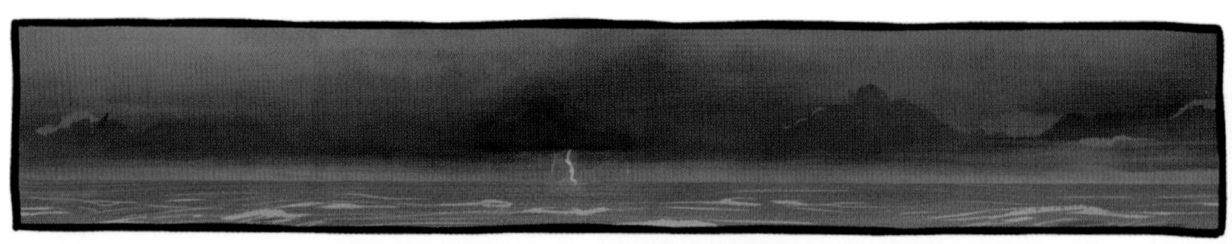

I HATE TO SAY, CHAR. BUT THIS STORM SNUCK RIGHT UP ON US.
WELL, NO POINT IN DELAYING THE INEVITABLE.

RING-A-BOT
22A
ATTENTION, ISLAND FEST.
TICKETS
A SEVERE WEATHER WARNING HAS BEEN ISSUED FOR THIS AFTERNOON.

THE CARNIVAL WILL CLOSE IN ONE HOUR.
HIGH WINDS ARE EXPECTED. ALL VENDORS, MAKE SURE YOUR BOOTHS ARE PROPERLY LOCKED DOWN.
THE FILM FESTIVAL WILL REMAIN ON SCHEDULE FOR THIS EVENING.

WHEEL O' PIE
I CAN'T BELIEVE THIS.
THERE GOES OUR FUNDRAISER.

HOW MANY TICKETS HAVE YOU TWO SOLD?
COME ON, LEX. WE'VE ONLY BEEN OPEN AN HOUR.

LEX!
DIDN'T YOU HEAR?
MY MOM CLOSED THE CARNIVAL.

I KNOW.
THE MOVIE FEST IS STILL ON. WHERE'S YOUR CREW?
DAGGETT
3

THAT I DON'T KNOW.
LOST 'EM, HUH? WELL, WE HAVEN'T SEEN THEM.

THAT'S BECAUSE THEY WENT TO THE CLUBHOUSE.

LEMON MERINGUE
BOSTON CREAM
DAGGETT

CLUBHOUSE?
I DIDN'T KNOW BRIAR WAS INTO GOLF.
MUD PIE
TICKETS
CASH

EXCUSE US, LADIES.
WE NEED TO CHAT IN PRIVATE.
PEANUT BUTTER
CHERRY
LEMON MERINGUE
BOSTON CREME

OK, SO . . . I HADN'T SEEN GAYLE SINCE THE WHARF.
THEN THIS MORNING, SHE AN' MADDIE SHOW UP. THEY SAY THEY WANT TO FINISH THE MOVIE.

THEY SAY THEY FOUND ATWOOD'S CLUBHOUSE.
I TOLD THEM, NO WAY, I WAS OUT!

SO THEN THEY STOLE MY CAMERA.

DAMMIT, ELIJAH!

I TOLD YOU THAT GIRL MADDIE WAS **CRAZY.**

LOOK . . . IT SEEMS LIKE YOU KNOW SOMETHING.
I DON'T CARE HOW OR WHY YOU KNOW IT.

I JUST NEED TO FIND THEM.

THE CLUBHOUSE.
YOU WON'T FIND IT ALONE.

I'M GOING WITH YOU.

IT'S A DEAL.
COME ON, MY MOTORBIKE IS BACK AT THE HOTEL.

ARE YOU KIDDING ME?
I'M DRIVING.

CLICK

LEX?
WHAT DO WE DO WITH ALL THESE PIES?
MUD PIE
TICKETS
CASH

ISLAND FES
AUGUST 29th - 31st
EDGARTOWN BANK

STONE PILLARS

BE CAREFUL,
DON'T SLIP!

16 · 8 · 4 · 1.9

16 · 8 · 4 · 1.9

16 · 8 · 4 · 1.9

IT LOOKS LIKE WE'RE NOT THE FIRST TO FIND THIS PLACE.

DOESN'T MATTER.

WE'LL BE THE FIRST TO BRING IT BACK.

HERE'S YOUR SCRIPT.
HEY . . .
DID YOU CHANGE THE ENDING?

I DON'T REMEMBER ANY OF THIS —
TRUST YOUR DIRECTOR AND JUST READ IT!

AS CAPTAIN LEVITT ATWOOD'S FORTUNE GREW, HE INVESTED IN HIS BELOVED ISLAND.
TAVERN

MUCH OF MARTHA VINEYARD'S CHARM CAN BE TRACED BACK TO HIS GENEROSITY.

WHOA.
IS THIS STUFF ALL TRUE?
KEEP READING.

DESPITE ALL HE HAD, THE CAPTAIN WAS NOT CONTENT UNTIL HE HAD BUILT A HOME . . .

FOR HIS AILING WIFE, ESTHER, AND THEIR NEWBORN DAUGHTER.

FAR FROM THE HORRORS OF HIS CLUBHOUSE, ATWOOD PURCHASED LAND ON THE SERENE EASTERN SHORELINE IN THE TOWN OF OAK BLUFFS.
BELIEVING A VIEW OF THE OCEAN WOULD REVERSE ESTHER'S POOR HEALTH, ATWOOD ASKED HIS BUILDERS TO CREATE A WALL OF WINDOWS FACING THE WATER.
BUT THE SEA WOULD NOT SAVE HER.
ON THEIR LAST DAY TOGETHER, THE CAPTAIN AND HIS WIFE WATCHED THE SUNRISE . . .
IN THE DAWNING LIGHT, HE TRIED TO PUT HER MIND AT PEACE . . .
AND SHARED THE ONLY WORDS THAT CAME TO MIND . . .

"There is no sight like that of the Grand Atlantic."

I KNOW THOSE WORDS.
THEY'RE ON THE FIREPLACE AT LEX'S HOTEL.

WHAT A COINCIDENCE.

YOU KNEW?

SURE DID. KEEP READING.

AFTER HIS WIFE'S DEATH, LEVITT ATWOOD REFUSED TO ENTER THE HOUSE.

HE FELL INTO A DESPAIR, AND AFTER A GREAT STORM, HE DISAPPEARED ALTOGETHER.

HIS DAUGHTER, CHARLOTTE, WAS RAISED BY THE HOUSEMAIDS.

CHARLOTTE FELL IN LOVE WITH AN ISLAND CARPENTER NAMED WINSTON DAGGETT.
HE USED HER FORTUNE TO TURN THEIR QUIET HOME INTO ONE OF THE COUNTRY'S FIRST LUXURY HOTELS.
THE GRAND ATLANTIC BROUGHT MUCH JOY TO ITS GUESTS, BUT THE STORIES OF HER FATHER'S CLUBHOUSE HAUNTED CHARLOTTE.
SHE SPENT THE REST OF HER LIFE ERASING HIS NAME.

CHARLOTTE DAGGETT DIED AT THE AGE OF 98, CONFIDENT SHE HAD WIPED THE NAME "CAPTAIN LEVITT ATWOOD" FROM ALL PUBLIC RECORD . . .

"BUT THAT IS NOW SO LONG AGO THAT THE HILLS HAVE FORGOTTEN THEM, THOUGH A SHADOW STILL LIES ON THE LAND."

ALL RIGHT, I ADMIT,
THAT LAST BIT I STOLE FROM TOLKIEN, BUT THE REST IS MINE.

LEX IS AN ATWOOD.
AND THIS MOVIE IS YOUR REVENGE.

WELL, LET'S CALL IT A RECKONING.

WHATEVER YOU WANNA CALL IT, MADDIE!
WE CAN'T DO THIS TO HER.

HEY.
THIS IS THE PRIZE-WINNING STORY THAT I PROMISED YOU.

AND DON'T PRETENED YOU WOULDN'T LIKE TO SEE HER FALL.
HEY, I DON'T HATE LEX!

OH NO?
DID YOU EVER FIND OUT WHO CALLED THE POLICE THAT NIGHT AT THE WHARF?

NO, YOU DIDN'T.
YOU WANTED IT TO BE LEX.
SLOW NO WAKE

YOU WANTED IT SO BAD . . .
YOU COULDN'T SEE IT WAS ME.

MADDIE?
I KNOW.
THE TRUTH HURTS.

"BLUE STREAK" THE DISGRACED HERO

"GHASTLY MADDIE" THE EXILED MONSTER

"CAPTAIN LEX" THE VILLAIN'S HEIR

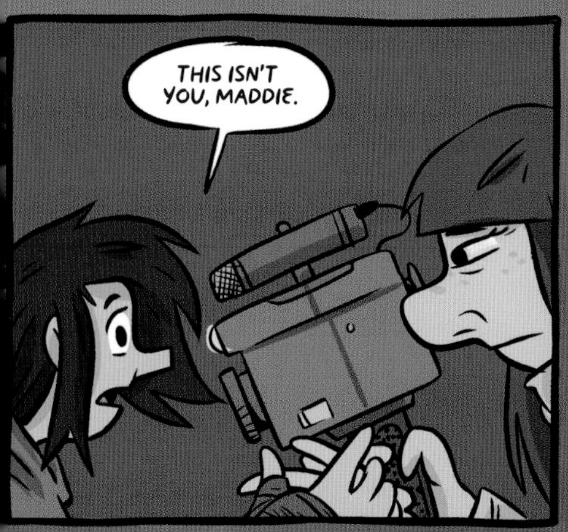
THIS ISN'T
YOU, MADDIE.

THIS ISN'T WHO I SPENT
THE SUMMER WITH.

I WANT THAT
GIRL BACK.

SHE WAS
MY FRIEND.

GAYLE . . .
DID I GO TOO FAR?

NO, MADDIE. WE CAME HERE FOR AN ENDING.

LIKE YOU SAID: "NO SPECIAL EFFECTS. NO GIMMICKS."

JUST TURN THE CAMERA ON.

DAGGETT
AT WOOD
LEVIT
SO LONG
THAT

MADISON GREY!

WHAT DID YOU DO TO GAYLE?

NOTHING.

GET OFF!

WHAT IS SHE DOING OUT THERE?

STOP HER, ELIJAH. SHE'LL LISTEN TO YOU.
ARE YOU KIDDING?

YOU CAN'T STOP HER.
SHE NEEDS TO FINISH THE MOVIE.

WELL, I'M GOING TO CHANGE HER MIND.

HE CONFRONTED THE SEA
WHO HAD BETRAYED HIM.
AND WHILE THE STORM
DROWNED OUT HIS WORDS . . .

HIS DESPAIR
WAS RESOUNDING.
AS IF IN RESPONSE . . .

A GIANT PHANTOM SHARK ROSE UP BEFORE HIM.

WHERE WERE YOU WHEN I NEEDED YOU?

I'M SORRY.
I SHOULD HAVE BEEN THERE.

IT'S NOT TOTALLY YOUR FAULT.
I WAS TOO SCARED TO ASK.

PLEASE, GAYLE.
LET'S GO HOME.

EASY FOR YOU TO SAY, THIS IS YOUR ISLAND.

HEY, LEX. DO YOU EVER WONDER IF IT'S REAL?

WHAT?
THE SHARK. I WONDER ABOUT IT SOMETIMES.

DOES IT REALLY KNOW THE PEOPLE WE'VE HURT?

I WONDER . . .

WILL IT COME FOR ME?

LIKE IT CAME FOR HIM?

NO FREAKING WAY.

GAYLE
SAVE ME.

SAVE ME

UNTIL THE STORM PASSES, WE'RE TRAPPED OUT HERE.

FOLLOW ME.

COME ON, LEX.

CRACK

HEY . . .

WHERE DID YOU GO?!

HEY—

CRACK

SAVE ME

ALEXANDRIA

ALEXANDRIA

ALEXANDRIA!

GET UP!
I CAN'T.

FINE.

OOF!
I'LL CARRY YOU.
CRACK

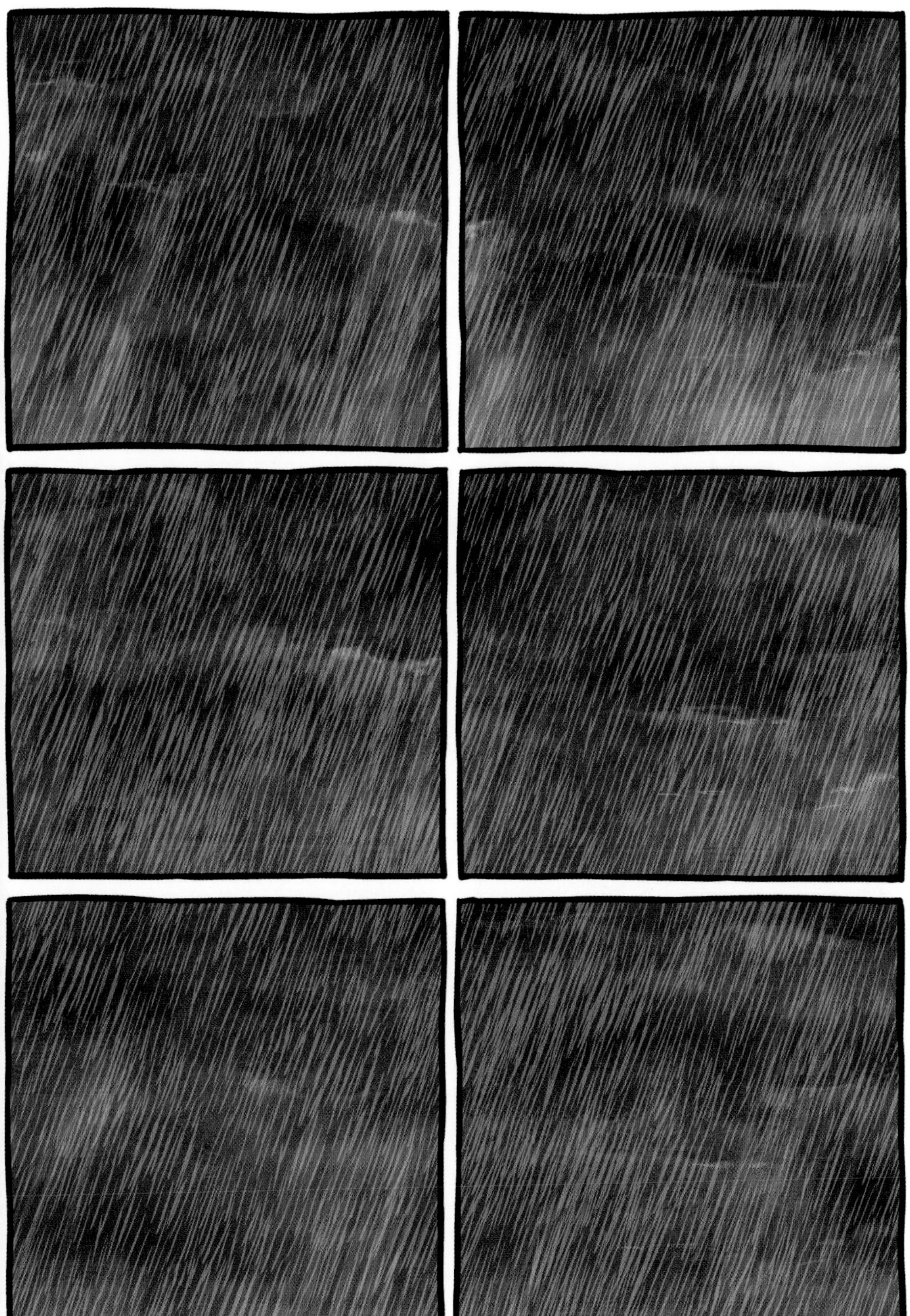

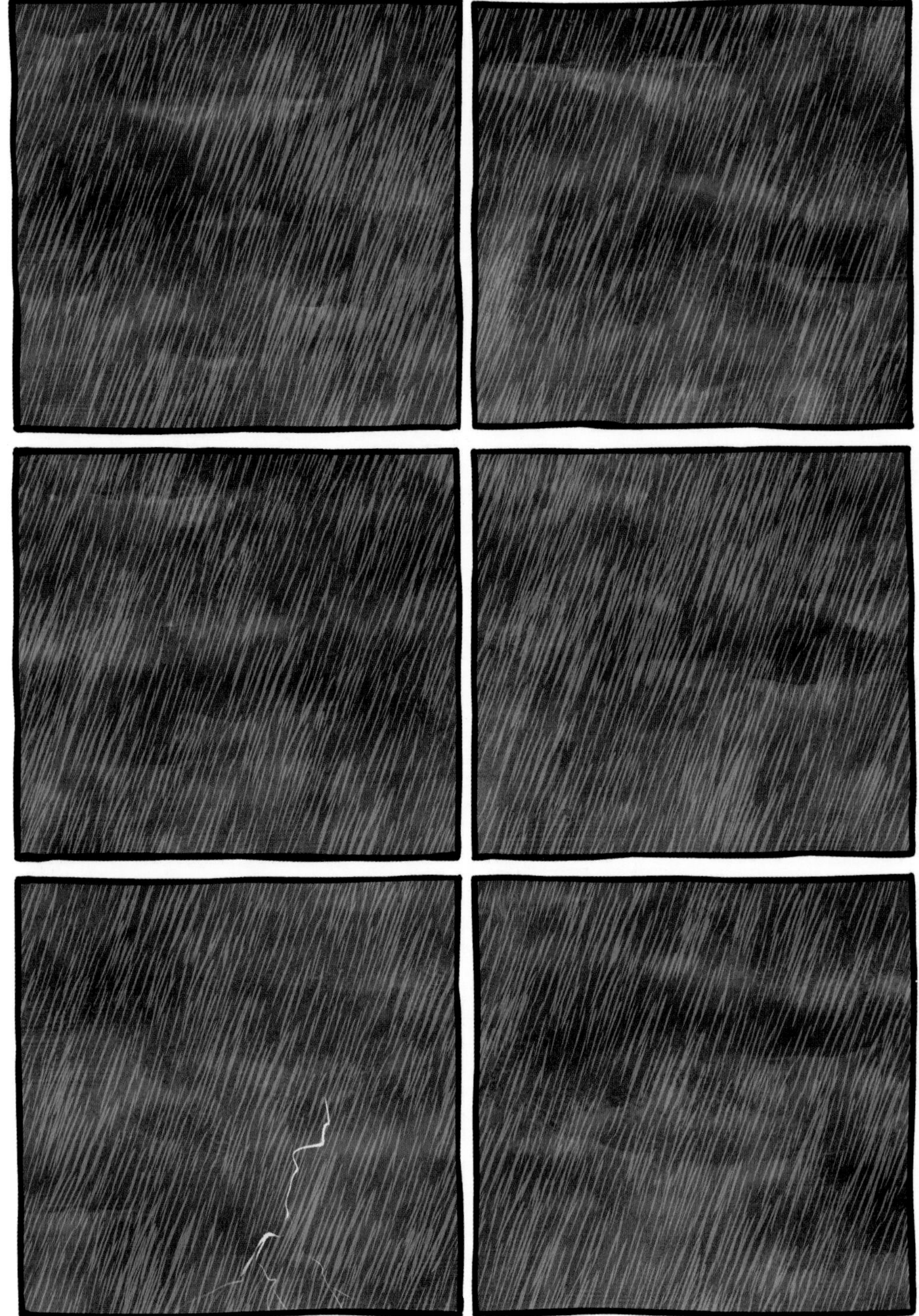

RUMBLE

ZANUCK

AUGUST 29TH - 31ST

AH.

HEY.

I'M SORRY, I STOLE YOUR —

CAMERA.

YOU KNOW . . .
I THINK YOU SAVED MY LIFE.

YOU SAVED MY BEST FRIEND.
LET'S CALL IT EVEN.

ELIJAH, WHAT DID WE GET?

WE GOT EVERYTHING.

NO, YOU DIDN'T. THERE IS MORE.

DOCUMENTS.
PHOTOGRAPHS.
THINGS MY GREAT-GRANDMOTHER COULDN'T STAND TO PART WITH.

MY MOM KEEPS THEM LOCKED UP. I CAN SHOW YOU.

LEX?
WHY WOULD YOU DO THAT?

I'M SICK OF BEING AFRAID.

WHAT DO YOU WANT TO DO?
IF WE TELL ATWOOD'S STORY . . .
HE GETS TO COME BACK.

I WANT TO LEAVE HIM RIGHT WHERE WE FOUND HIM.
BUT IT CAN'T BE MY DECISION.

WE'RE A TEAM.

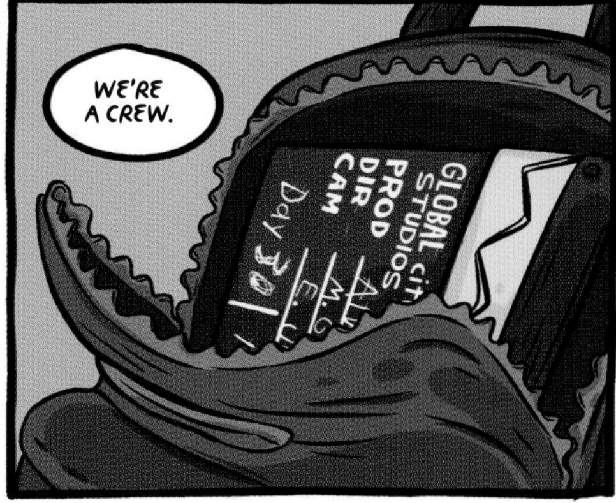
WE'RE A CREW.
GLOBAL
STUDIOS
PROD
DIR
CAM
Day

WHATEVER WE CALL IT.
WE DECIDE TOGETHER.

LEAVE HIM.

WELL?

FINE WITH ME.

YEAH, DEFINITELY.

ZODAK
VIBRA-COLOR

UM...
ANYONE HAVE A LIGHTER?
I DON'T.
NOPE.

ARG!!

IT'S GOING TO BE OK, LEX.

I...

I DON'T KNOW WHAT HAPPENS NOW.

WE GET TO START OVER.

DAGGETT
3

SQUAWK

HA!

EPILOGUE

GAYLE, IF I FALL IN THE WATER, YOU'RE IN BIG TROUBLE.

TRUST ME, MOM. JUST A LITTLE FARTHER.

BLACK CAT CREAMERY
HOMEMADE FLAVORS
FRESH FRUIT
FLAVORS
VINEYARD SWEETS
OK, I'M GOING TO LOSE IT FOR A SECOND.
YOU DESERVE IT, MOM.
HOW . . . HOW THE HECK DID YOU DO THIS?

WITH HELP FROM YOUR LOCAL HARDWARE STORE, OF COURSE.
WE ISLANDERS HAVE TO STICK TOGETHER.
CONES

SORRY WE'RE LATE!

I HOPE YOU DON'T MIND, AUDREY.
I BROUGHT A FEW THINGS OVER.

NOTHING TOO FANCY.
FROM YOU, CHAR? I EXPECT NOTHING LESS.

CONGRATULATIONS.
THANK YOU.
AUDREY!

YOU KNOW, WHEN I WAS A KID, THIS WAS A TACKLE SHOP.
LLOYD'S BAIT! I REMEMBER THAT!

THANKS FOR COMING.

WOULDN'T MISS IT.
NO ELIJAH, HUH?

AFTER SHARK! WRAPPED, HIS DAD HAD TO GET BACK TO BOSTON.

FRESH FRUIT
70¢
$1.50

MMM...

OH MY GOD.
IT'S A CUSTOMER.

OH, HELLO.
HI.

MOM! GET OVER HERE!
OH MY GOD.

HM . . .
TWO SCOOPS OF ELDERBERRY OUTBURST.

TWO SCOOPS.
COMING RIGHT UP.

GOOD EVENING, YOU MUST BE THE OTHER MS. BRIAR.
MR. JONES?

YOU'RE STILL HERE!

I TOLD DAD WE NEEDED TO STAY ONE MORE DAY.

I MADE A DEAL I COULDN'T BREAK.

READY, SON?

HUH?

READY, DAD!
LITE-SCREEN

PLEASE HAVE A SEAT, EVERYONE!
THE MOVIE IS ABOUT TO BEGIN.

WHAT MOVIE?

SHARK SUMMER
A FILM BY
ELIJAH JONES

GOOD TITLE.
THANKS.

2074
Terror

02074
PROD Atwood Terror
DIR M. Grey
CAM E. Jones
Day 32 | take 9

CHUM
MP!

THE END?!
a BABY GOATS production

I WENT TO SEE CHARLIE AND HE REMINDED ME . . .
TO MAKE A MOVIE, YOU NEED TO FIND A STORY WORTH TELLING.

JUST SOMETIMES, IT'S NOT THE ONE YOU WERE LOOKING FOR.

ELIJAH JONES. UP-AND-COMING FILMMAKER.
IMPRESSIVE.

OH BOY, AM I REALLY GONNA MISS YOU TWO.

HAVE THEY TALKED SINCE THE STORM?
I DON'T THINK SO.

GO SAY SOMETHING.

I CAN'T.
NOT TONIGHT.

THE LONGER YOU WAIT, THE FURTHER YOU'LL HAVE TO GO.

JUST SAYING.

HI.
HEY.

JUST WAITING FOR MY MOM.

I DON'T WANT TO RUSH HER.

HOW'S PRACTICE?

EH, YOU KNOW.
YEAH.

I HEARD JULIA IS PITCHING.

SHE'S NOT BAD ACTUALLY.

SHE MUST HAVE BEEN WATCHING YOU.

HA HA, I'M SURE SHE WOULD NOT WANT TO HEAR THAT.

AH, HEY, I WAS WONDERING . . .

DO YOU WANT TO GO INTO THE CITY WITH ME ON SATURDAY?

WE COULD, LIKE, HANG OUT ON NEWBURY STREET.
OH.

I SHOULD ASK MY MOM IF SHE NEEDS ME.

BUT IT'S PROBABLY FINE.

IT'D BE FUN TO GET OFF THE ISLAND FOR A DAY.
EXACTLY WHAT I WAS THINKING.